GABRIELLE MARIE KOZAK

Trooper A3

Exterminate

For every scientist who faces the conflict of science and justice.
For every child who feels lost and alone.
And for every young adult whose future doesn't look like what they hoped it would be.

Contents

prologue

He's just a farm boy—well, a man—but he's spent his entire life of twenty years on a farm somewhere in southern Africa where modern technology is virtually nonexistent. He's a tour guide now, around Victoria Falls. He considered it a step up from the dry boredom of farm life. Something to be proud of. But here he is, tangling with some nightmare from the African jungle in the first week of his new job. He tells himself dimly that he's going back home.

If he even survives this.

He's scared stiff. The big cat is right on top of him, playing with him now. He tried fighting the cat at first, a horrifying prospect. He's been clawed and bitten, multiple times, even if he had succeeded in giving the leopard what seemed to be a mere scratch with the knife he happened to be carrying. But now that the wildcat has eliminated the threat—well, what it seemed to consider only an irritation—it is content to merely roll its prey back and forth in the long African grass, scaring the daylights out of its toy.

But that isn't what's bothering the man now. He's become acutely aware of a new, inflaming pain.

He was just bleeding so heavily that he thought he was going to die. But now he feels his strength coming back to him—and, with it, an unbearable pain that burns like fire, everywhere. He screams.

He's all alone, though, except for the leopard. No one has bothered to stick around to see whether he survived or not. It's too dangerous, and besides no one cares about him—Ayan Monet.

But why should they? he asks himself suddenly with a vehemence that makes him wonder if he'd heard the question aloud. He's just a stupid farmer kid who's never even finished high school. He's literally worked his heart out trying to get somewhere, but failed. Nobody wanted him. So he'd come here. And look at him now. A leopard's snack. Or maybe just its toy. He wants to scream again, but it's just about now that he realizes the wildcat is losing interest. Ayan hardly dares breathe.

After batting the young man's face a few times with velveted paws, the leopard apparently decides the human is dead. It didn't mean to do that. After breathing down his neck—literally—it growls. Still nothing. So it stalks off in a state of high dudgeon.

Within minutes, however, the form stirs.

Ayan is still alive.

He moans, sitting up slowly as he realizes all of his various cuts and scrapes are closing up. Healing. Leaving scars—purple scars.

What?

He shakes his head dizzily against the burning fire in his veins. He wishes it would stop. It's going to drive him insane.

He must not be seeing right, he decides. Somehow he gets to his feet, and looks around him. It is almost night, and the sun is setting. There is no one around, but he knows where the village is. Or he thinks he does. Can he get there?

Ayan stumbles towards the setting sun, his walk unsteady. His blood burns. It won't stop. He feels it getting to his head, and he fights the insane feeling desperately. He just has to get to the village. There'll be a doctor there; they can fix him up. And then he will go back home. And stay there.

* * *

When he wakes up, he isn't the same. He can dimly remember what's happened to him as a doctor asks him all sorts of things. The doctor says he's fine—perfectly fine. But Ayan knows he isn't. The pain is still there. He tries explaining it, but he can't. Eventually the doctor leaves.

Ayan gets somewhat better, used to the pain, used to being ten times as strong as everyone around him. But he doesn't go home. He has one thing he wants to do now: find and kill that leopard.

one

I t was the end of an ordinary late-autumn class day at Harvard University, Cambridge, Massachusetts. The students were eager to disperse in the college grounds and eventually find their way to their respective homes, or the college dormitories—at least, those who didn't have the bother of an additional lecture that afternoon.

On one of the college paths, winding through a grove of flowering, uniform-sized trees, two of these students were walking. Well, more than two. But two stood out, though it was obvious they were trying not to. It was just as obvious that they were siblings, though they looked more like friends. And they were so full of life that it created a vibrantly cheerful atmosphere around them.

One of them, the taller and older one, was a young man, about twenty years old. He had thick dark brown hair that spilled out over his forehead from underneath the hood of his dark blue sweater. Underneath it he wore a bluish gray shirt, and his pants were a darker hue of the same color. He wore blue running shoes as well. On his face was a pair of tinted glasses. He looked very athletic, and those who knew him were well aware that his appearances did not deceive. He was in his third year of college.

On the other hand, his companion, a pretty eighteen-year-old brunette and equally, unmistakably athletic, was a college freshman. She wore tall leather boots, and a bright yellow dress with a light purple shawl. She was talking to her older brother, but also typing on her cell phone at the same time. They were engaged in a rather serious conversation concerning schoolwork.

"French, lesson six, all exercises." The girl scowled. "Why do they do this to us?"

"Hey, we go to Harvard, if you didn't notice," the boy returned casually. "And it was your choice to take French. I have told you that...thirty-three times? And this is your thirty-third day of college, isn't it," he added thoughtfully.

"Well, I'm not taking it next year," his younger sister sniffed.

"Anyway, it can't be as bad as psychology," the young man went on. "I might be smarter than 99 percent of my class, but even I have trouble with that one. So there, Kit."

"Psychology is a more extraordinary thing to take than French," Kit retorted. "Why does Dad want you taking it, anyway—*Arthur?*"

For some reason, Arthur pulled a face. "Search me." He shrugged helplessly. "But why not? Imagine if I were to take accounting."

Kit shook her head. "You nut."

"The name's Arthur Foley," he told her gravely with a look of injured dignity.

She shook her head, giggling. Putting her phone into her pocket, she pointed at a car ahead. "Hey, there's Uncle Jason!"

Seeing that she looked ready to run ahead to the vehicle that waited on the side of the street, Arthur grinned. "Think he'll wait?"

Kit laughed. "No."

"Well, I guess there's only one way to find out," Arthur murmured, continuing to walk at his slow, leisurely pace.

His sister shook her head again. "Whatever—I'm leaving," she added, breaking into an easy run that would have been considered fast by the average person but seemed quite effortless to her.

Arthur smiled after her, watching her go as he plodded along. She got to the car hundreds of feet ahead of him, casting a single glance back before she slipped into the passenger seat and slammed the door behind her. Arthur ran his hands through his hair, then suddenly leaped forward into a run as the car began to pull away from the curb without him.

"Hey!" he shouted, bolting after the car. He ran even faster than the girl had, chasing the car in desperation. And he was almost touching it when the driver suddenly increased speed, leaving Arthur grasping at the air.

Gritting his teeth, he kept up with the car, ignoring the startled looks he got from pedestrians around him. Finally, the car stopped, and Arthur tumbled into the back seat, panting.

Kit glanced back at him, highly amused. She was laughing again. "I told you so. But you hit eighty miles an hour."

"Hi Uncle," Arthur gasped out, ignoring his sister as he pulled his backpack off his back and let it fall onto the seat.

The man behind the wheel smiled. No older than twenty-five, he looked quite young, with light brown hair and cheerful gray-brown eyes.

"Hi," he returned. "Get your seat belt on, Arty."

"It's not Arty," Arthur mumbled, but he buckled his seat belt anyway.

Seconds later, the car was in motion again, and they were presumably on their way home. It wasn't long before the driver asked the two younger adults how school had gone, with an air of routine.

"Oh, fine, fine," Kit told him, leaning back in her seat boredly after a failed attempt to put her feet up on the dashboard. "The usual. We tell you that every time, Uncle Jason."

"I don't know what 'usual' means, you know," Jason returned in an injured tone. "I never went to college. I was a street kid."

"Mhmm, we know," Arthur grinned from the back seat. "It's alright. Just like normal school."

"Except harder," Kit put in. "Much harder."

"And you've already told me that as well," Jason growled. The two laughed.

"So, Arthur," their uncle went on, "where do we go for the eye appointment again? It's been so long I forgot."

For some reason, even though he was wearing glasses, Arthur reacted in an unimaginable way. He began to cough, and splutter, and even choke. Kit glanced back at him sympathetically.

"You're so funny, Uncle Jason," Arthur managed finally, brushing his sleeve across his face.

"Hospital?" Jason queried innocently.

Arthur shook his head emphatically, but before he could say anything else, Kit leaned forward in her seat and pointed towards the bridge they were about to cross. "Look!"

And the next moment, the car ahead of them abruptly lost control, shooting off the bridge into the water below.

<h1 style="text-align:center">two</h1>

J ason slammed on the brakes. Kit gasped in horror, and as their car came to a stop, Arthur's hand was already on the door handle. So was Kit's, and so was Jason's, the moment he took it off the wheel.

An instant later the three sprang out of the car to the edge of the bridge, Arthur in the lead. Glancing briefly at the twisted metal barrier where the car had gone through, he turned his attention to the vehicle that was now rapidly sinking into the river. Arthur had good ears, and he could hear someone—multiple someones—screaming for help.

Without a moment's hesitation, he vaulted over the railing and into the water, Jason and Kit close behind him. Though jumping off bridges was generally considered something dangerous and potentially suicidal, he came up some distance away from the car, perfectly fine and swimming frantically to get to the unfortunate vehicle. Finally, it seemed—though it took him only seconds—he reached it, and glanced through the windows at the one, two, three—five people inside.

It was the boy and girl who were screaming. Water was rushing in through a crack in the windshield, and the three adults in the car—two women and a man—were trying desperately to get the doors open before the car was completely submerged. The waterway wasn't that deep, but it was deeper than the car was tall.

Arthur grabbed hold of the outside handle of the passenger-side door and jerked it open. The older woman stared at him in shock as water poured into the car now. She looked about forty.

"Out! Out! Everybody out!" Arthur yelled as he went on to get a side door open. The boy had been watching him, but now he was struggling with his younger sister's car seat, trying to get her out of it. By the time Arthur got the door open, the boy had her in his arms, ready to go, even if she was screaming at the top of her lungs. He shoved her out the door at Arthur.

Arthur grabbed the little girl, wrapping one of his strong arms around her waist as he struck out and up for shore with the other. Above him, people were yelling encouragement, crowding around the edge of the bridge.

"What's your name?" he asked as he made his way to land. He was having no trouble swimming, even with her, but he was worried that she was in too much shock—he wanted to make her talk. But she didn't say anything. Just started shivering in the cold water.

"It's Dawn," panted a young voice from behind him. It was the twelve-year-old. He was swimming as well.

Arthur smiled briefly as he touched ground. He wished he'd kicked his shoes off; they were waterlogged. But at least they weren't boots like Kit's.

Two seconds later, the firm ground was beneath Arthur's feet. Water squelched out of his shoes as he carried Dawn a short distance and gently lowered her to the ground, shouting for someone to get a blanket.

He checked her over quickly while he waited, really seeing her over for the first time. She was chubby, with curly red hair. But people were crowding around. He had to tell them to get away and give her room to breathe.

Someone had blankets, and Arthur wrapped the little girl in one and dried off her hair while the girl's brother got to shore. He was panting, but otherwise fine, besides being completely soaked. Arthur handed one of the blankets to the boy, too. His hair was thick and curly like his sister's, but more copper, and his eyes were green. His cheeks were flushed from swimming in cold water, and he'd lost one of his shoes in the adventure.

"Is she okay?" he asked Arthur anxiously.

Arthur nodded. "I think so."

The boy managed a weak smile. "Thanks."

Behind him, Arthur could see Kit emerging from the water with the younger woman, who seemed so cold and shocked that she had had trouble getting to land on her own. Kit glanced at Arthur briefly.

"Jason wants your help with the car," she told him quickly.

Arthur realized that Jason was waving at him from the water while the last two of the car's passengers made their own way to shore. He sighed, nodding. "Okay. Be back."

With that, he ran back into the water, disregarding the towel someone offered him. He fought his way back to where the car was going down with the strength and energy of an Olympic swimmer, reaching his uncle within seconds.

Jason was waiting for someone to toss him a rope from the bridge, which they did just as Arthur got to him. He smiled momentarily at Arthur, and then ducked underwater with the rope to attach it to the car somewhere before it could sink further. After taking the time to fill his lungs with air, Arthur followed him down, but too late to be of any use. He popped up again a moment after Jason did, on the other side of the car.

"Got it?" Arthur shouted to him. Above them, the crowds were cheering.

Jason nodded silently, spitting out a large quantity of water. "Get onto the bridge," he ordered once he could speak. "Don't lose the rope. That thing is full of water," he added, just in time before a wave came and filled his mouth again.

Without wasting breath on an answer, Arthur started for the shore again, slightly annoyed that Jason hadn't needed his help there after all. When he got to land this time, however, he realized he'd lost his glasses. He took a moment to glance at the small family—paramedics were showing up now—before he started for the bridge. But then he heard a startled, half-hysterical exclamation from behind him, in a strangely familiar voice, and froze.

"Evolet Whyte!" It was the eighteen-year-old girl. "Jaz! Oh wow! You guys! Jason! I had no clue you Whytes were around here! Are you still superhuman? Oh wow guys thanks so much!"

Evolet Whyte, aka Arthur Foley, stood still in horror as his cover was blown for all the world to see. And then a camera flashed in his face, and he jumped, and wheeled around to glance at his sister, Jasmine, formerly known as Kit, who was looking aghast.

"Jaz, shut her up!" he gritted, realizing that the young lady they'd rescued was Livia Parson—Jasmine's best friend in middle school, whom they'd lost contact with in recent years. She'd seen his purple eyes, and the memories had clicked.

Jasmine's light blue eyes met her older brother's purple ones, and she nodded seriously, then turned to Livia in a desperate effort to keep her quiet. Evolet shook himself out of his stupor and began to shove his way through the ever-increasing crowd to the bridge.

But as he went, he realized it was too late. Cameras were flashing, reporters were arriving, people were talking and taking pictures with their phones—

"Oh joy," he muttered under his breath, shutting his eyes—much to the disappointment of an amateur cameraman—and charging towards the bridge, heedless of who was in his way.

He found the man who had tied the rope securely to the back of his pickup truck, and surveyed him seriously. The man looked trustworthy, though as excited as the rest.

"You got the car?" Evolet demanded breathlessly.

"Yeah, sure I got it, it's good," the man blurted out. "Hey, are you really a Whyte? Man, that's—"

He broke off, looking crestfallen as Evolet ignored everything after the "yeah" and swung around, waving to his sister and uncle.

"It's blown!" he shouted to them. "We gotta go *now!*"

three

Hours later, after taking a shower to wash the river water out of his hair, Evolet headed into the kitchen of Jason's home in Cambridge to make himself a cup of hot chocolate—and some for the others, if they wanted any. He found his uncle sitting at the table, reading something on his cell phone. Jason looked up as Evolet came into the room.

Evolet caught the serious look in the older man's eyes, and frowned. "Well?"

Jason shook his head despondently. "It's blown up."

"Huh?" Evolet's eyebrows shot up.

"The news has gone all over," Jason explained, sighing. "It's hopeless."

"So Cambridge knows?" Evolet asked quietly. "About Jaz and me?"

Jason did a facepalm. "Are you kidding me? The *world* knows," he told his nephew emphatically, "that you and Jaz, also known as Arthur and Kit Foley, have been going to Harvard University under an assumed name! It's all over the internet! Welcome to 2048!"

"Blast," Evolet mumbled.

He set a small pot of water to boil, then went back to his room to collect his half-dry clothes for washing. Heading down the hallway into the garage, where Jason and his niece and nephew always did their laundry, he found Jasmine already there, putting her own clothes into the washer.

"It's all over the internet, Jason says," he told her quietly as she held the washer lid open for him. "We try so hard to stay anonymous—got an AKA and everything—convinced the college to keep it a dead secret—and then we run into your friend and everything goes *bang!*"

Jasmine half-shrugged. "It's not her fault," she replied shortly. "She didn't know. She apologized."

"What, you're talking to her?" Evolet gaped.

His younger sister nodded, smiling slightly. "We exchanged phone numbers—that's a plus. You'll never guess why she's in town."

"Spy mission on the Whytes," Evolet muttered.

Shaking her head, Jasmine slapped his arm lightly. "Snap out of it. Nothing as exciting as that. She's just visiting her cousins—the kids we rescued."

"Oh yeah," Evolet remembered. "Dawn and…?"

"Michael Leblanc," Jasmine returned. "Dawn's deaf, too."

Finally Evolet managed a bit of a smile. "Well, good thing we were around then, I guess. But seriously! Everyone is going to know who we are now. And we can't do any undercover lifesaving on the side if people know that there are superhumans in town! It's just too obvious."

"Deal with it," Jasmine told him bluntly.

He stared at her, his mouth hanging open. "This was your idea."

"Okay, well, it's gone and done now, so who cares?" Jasmine shrugged again. "I'd like a hot chocolate, too, please."

"How'd you know I was making one?" her brother demanded.

Jasmine rolled her eyes. "Think I can't hear you?"

* * *

Evolet couldn't fall asleep that night. He was too busy thinking of his and Jasmine's college life—of the precautions they'd taken to remain unknown and what would happen now that everyone would recognize them for who they truly were.

They'd liked the popularity a bit when they were younger. The entire Whyte family had become famous after defeating Zaire and his Victors in early 2042. But it had gotten tiring to go outside and not be able to do anything without being pestered about autographs, photos, and the like. So when Evolet graduated from the high school in Annapolis, he'd decided to go to Harvard—incognito.

He and his parents had managed the paperwork—with Jason Foley's help. It had been decided that since Jason already lived in Cambridge, Evolet could live with him there instead of staying at the college dormitory, which would help keep his fellow classmates' eyes off him.

And so he'd become Arthur Foley, and been that person for two years—closing in on three. Jasmine had decided to join him, though her twin sister Alison was going to a college in Nebraska.

Evolet and Jasmine loved being able to go places without being recognized as Whytes and superhumans. And an added benefit was that, during their spare time, they could do vigilante work. No one knew that it was the two "Fosters."

But all that was going to change now, he reflected grimly. If they were lucky, they'd get away without being "blamed" for all the prevented murders, impossible rescues, and the like in the last two years. But if they did any of that now—

He sighed, feeling a bit sorry for Jasmine. He, Evolet, could finish college this year, if he wanted to—and so could Jasmine, but she wouldn't get credit for all the years that Evolet had.

He didn't know. They could stay until the year was finished. Or even leave before that, if they got desperate.

Evolet remembered the conversation he'd had with his dad over the phone that evening, after the incident. Conner had been surprised, but not really shocked.

"It was bound to come out sometime," he'd told Evolet. "At least you got two years of normal life again."

"At this point I guess you and Mom won't even have to dress up for the end-of-the-year ceremony," Evolet had told him, making him laugh.

"Well, don't tell Vi that, or she'll come in her purple jacket and everything," Conner had teased. The next moment, he'd yelped in annoyance. Presumably Violet Whyte was in the room with him, listening. She liked to do that.

Evolet smiled to himself, remembering. If there was one thing he missed about being in Annapolis, it was being with his parents and Aunt Moira. And Charles, too. He wasn't such a pain now, being fifteen, and everyone agreed that he looked much like his father, what with his blond hair and blue eyes. He was an okay type.

The twenty-year-old shook his head drowsily, telling himself to go to sleep. He'd need to be very awake tomorrow. And every day after that.

<h1 style="text-align:center">four</h1>

As Evolet had suspected, it was months before people stopped bothering them in the streets. But by the end of the school year, he had resigned himself to returning next year to finish college normally. So he sat in the auditorium with his classmates and Jasmine, watching the graduations and clapping at all the appropriate places. But that was tiring, and after an hour or so of it he whispered to Jasmine that he was going to head home. Other people were already leaving.

She was busy whispering to one of her friends, so she merely nodded, and Evolet walked away briskly, sneaking towards the back door. But he hadn't gotten halfway there before the person on the stage stopped speaking, and suddenly a terrified quiet fell over the entire auditorium, broken only by a sudden scream.

Evolet looked up and saw a nightmare.

There was a wildcat leaping at him out of nowhere. Evolet had a split second to think to himself that it was a leopard, before he cartwheeled to the side just in time to avoid the claws that threatened to score down his face. He landed on his feet, jumping away as the leopard pounced again, its mouth open in an earsplitting roar.

Evolet grabbed an empty chair, shoving it at the cat desperately as he backed into the aisle. The leopard batted it aside with a growl of anger and annoyance, and jumped a third time. Clenching his teeth, Evolet grabbed another chair—for some reason the chairs around him were quickly being vacated—and held it up to shield himself.

He did better than he expected, and gained a moment's respite as the cat's claws stuck in the wood. Throwing the chair aside with the leopard trying to disengage its paws, Evolet grabbed yet another and slammed it down on the leopard as hard as he possibly could.

The cat gave an agonized howl, and flipped over, suddenly freeing its claws. But then Evolet had his hands around its neck, feeling desperately for some sort of collar. He didn't find one, and was just about to leap away before the leopard could bite his hands off, when a voice rang out above the various screams and auditorium noises.

"Down, Giza!"

The leopard suddenly went tamely limp. Evolet didn't let go, but he glanced up, breathing a sigh of relief—and then catching his breath as he stared in shock.

The newcomer was tall and muscular, dressed in clothes that looked like they'd come from a charity drop off. He walked jerkily, his lips moving as if he was whispering to himself. His hair was thick, long, and messy—a literal patchwork of black and white. His eyes were a vivid coral color, with something in them that flashed insanely. His face and forearms were scarred horribly—the scars were, shockingly, purple.

He strolled up the aisle, as casually as a graduate, but he was scanning the rows of seats as he went. And then he looked up—and straight into Evolet's eyes.

They stared at each other a moment, sizing each other up. Because Evolet had already realized with the first moment of looking that this person belonged to the leopard which had just attacked him.

The man was here for the Whytes.

And he obviously recognized Evolet in turn, for now he threw his head back and smiled, laughing suddenly, a sound that electrified the already tense silence. Evolet saw people cringe. Someone was calling the cops. Perfect.

"Hello! You Evolet Whyte?" the man asked him slowly, in bad, French-accented English. Evolet nodded silently.

The man grinned hugely, waving his arms wildly. "I Ayan Monet."

"Nice to meet you," Evolet murmured tentatively.

Ayan pointed at the leopard, and then signaled to it. The big cat stood up fluidly and stalked over to his master, watching Evolet sullenly.

"My leopard, Giza, he sniff, he smell—superhumans," Ayan went on, beaming. "We been looking for you! You and other girl. Name Jasmine, 'think.'"

He paused reflectively, and then looked around him in awe—which suddenly melted into a horrifying kind of anger. "Fancy American college."

"Hey, do you want something?" Evolet asked. He gestured vaguely to the terrified people around them, though he felt just about as confused as they. "You're kind of interrupting," he told him pointedly, yet politely. "And— uhh—I don't think pets are allowed in school." He made a weak attempt to laugh.

"Not pet," Ayan shook his head emphatically. "Killer, bad. I kill it!" he added vehemently, reaching down to rub the top of the leopard's head, who purred.

Evolet blinked slowly, and then reached his own hand up in the very natural—for him—gesture of running his hand through his hair. "Oh." He turned slightly, wondering what to do next.

After taking a year of psychology, Evolet was 99 percent sure that the man standing a few feet away from him was completely insane, unless the bad English grammar had him confused. But it wasn't just that—it was the unfitting clothes, the atmosphere of danger, the wild eyes, and the constantly changing attitude—not to mention the leopard-petting. He glanced around briefly to see if anyone had a plan.

Someone met his eye and nodded slightly. "Police are on the way," he mouthed.

Evolet nodded back to them, relieved. So all he had to do was keep Ayan Monet and his leopard, Giza—if that was his name—out of trouble for the time being. It looked like Ayan was just there to talk to him, anyway—since he was superhuman—

What?

"LOOK OUT!" someone shrieked.

Evolet wheeled around, both to look Ayan over again and to "look out," only to see Ayan charging him without a word of warning. He stepped back, but too late—Ayan lunged. The older man landed directly on top of Evolet, with a shockingly hard impact that doubled Evolet's suspicions of "superhuman."

Even as he fought with Ayan, Evolet's mind raced.

He took a hard knock and surmised that Ayan was in good practice.

He returned it, and decided Ayan had to be superhuman and there was nothing else for it.

Seeing the patchwork-style hair and coral eyes, Evolet caught his breath both as Ayan screeched at him and he realized that the T5 superhuman strain was involved in this, somehow.

He shook off the feeling of unreality, reminding himself how the fight with Zaire had ended and that he didn't want this one to end like that, too. But he was getting worried that Ayan was—impossibly—hyper-T5, especially when they got locked into a position where both were straining their arm's strength against each other.

And then Ayan won. Yelling again in victory—he wasn't a quiet fighter—he shoved Evolet away from him, into the crowd of people that hadn't yet managed to evacuate the large building.

Evolet leaped onto some chairs and shouted to Ayan, trying to draw him away from the crowd. Ayan turned to look at him, and growled, much like Giza.

He jumped up as well, and proceeded to chase Evolet around the auditorium. It didn't end, even when police crowded into the building and tried to get the people flowing out steadily.

One of the cops shot a taser at Ayan. No effect.

Suddenly a chair that Evolet sprang onto tipped over unexpectedly.

He jumped for another chair, in front of a window, but that one fell over too. The next thing he knew, he was on the ground and cornered against the wall, with Ayan on top of him again.

Ayan grabbed a chair and raised it.

Evolet held up his hands in front of his face as a defense measure, but then suddenly someone jerked Ayan away and the chair with him.

The newcomer tossed the chair away, twisted Ayan's arms behind him expertly, and—before Ayan knew what was happening—launched him into the window.

Ayan shattered through it, landing on the glass-covered pavement outside and quickly finding himself surrounded by policemen.

Evolet took a deep breath, lying still for a moment as he tried to process what happened. Then he got up to meet the police—and find out who'd rescued him.

five

Evolet finally stood up, rubbing a deep, but quickly healing cut on his face ruefully as he wondered dismally if for some reason it might scar like Ayan's face had.

He jumped to attention suddenly as, outside the building, the seemingly stunned Ayan leaped up and away from the police who were trying to restrain him. The man shouted something in French to his leopard, and the two of them dashed away from the auditorium without a backward glance.

It took Evolet a moment to realize that Jasmine was standing next to him, panting and brushing her hands off. He was startled when she said his name— well, his baby name.

"Evy, who was he?" she asked him, chuckling as she realized he hadn't known she was there.

He shook his head. "Said his name was Ayan Monet. Was that French he spoke just now?"

She shrugged. "Sounded like it. Oh, look, the police want to talk to you."

Bewildered, Evolet swung his head around to see a sheriff standing on the other side of him, notepad in hand. The sheriff was obviously trying very hard to look serious, while failing miserably at keeping an expression of awe off his face.

"You're Evolet Whyte," he declared.

"Yes," Evolet nodded briefly, hoping this wasn't going to be a long and exhausting process. He sighed to himself.

"Who was the guy with the tiger—or leopard—whatever that was?"

"He called himself Ayan Monet," Evolet returned, as Jasmine murmured:

"Leopard."

The policeman arched an eyebrow as he took his notes. "And she is—?" he demanded, jerking his pencil in the direction of Jasmine. "Jasmine Whyte?"

"Yeah, that's Jaz," Evolet replied with an air of resignation.

"So, did you start the fight, or did Monet, or did it just happen all at once—"

"He started it," Jasmine broke in, sounding somewhat annoyed that her brother was even a suspect. "I mean Monet," she added hastily. "There were hundreds of witnesses."

"Right, right," the policeman mumbled, looking over his notes.

Then he glanced back up. "Did you guys know Monet before?"

* * *

"I've decided to stay out of crime," Evolet declared to his uncle and sister over dinner. "It's too stressful, and I get enough of interrogation as it is." He sighed ruefully.

"A healthy resolution," Jason nodded gravely. "So what were you saying in the car? Something I missed? And you've got a bandage on your face?" He smiled thoughtfully. "I've never seen any kind of bandage on you before, do you realize that?"

"I know! He looks so cute," Jasmine cut in brightly. "I'm going to send a picture to Mom."

Evolet buried his face in his hands, groaning. "It's not world news—"

"Actually, it is," Jason interrupted. "I already read what happened. So his name was Ayan Monet?"

"Right," Evolet nodded, somewhat relieved that he wasn't going to have to tell the whole story all over again—and Jason generally proved to be a better interrogator than the police.

"Thought so. I saw it there, but I forgot." Jason leaned forward slightly in his chair. "The cops probably told you this, but he's famous?"

"Famous?" Evolet and Jasmine echoed at the same time, then glared at each other.

Jason ignored them. "Yeah, famous. He's in that online encyclopedia—

listed as a notorious African criminal. Apparently he was literally traveling the African continent over and over again with his leopard, doing what he liked—till last autumn."

"What happened last autumn?" Jasmine wondered absentmindedly, clapping her hand over her mouth as she remembered—too late.

Evolet smacked himself in the forehead, reflecting gloomily a moment later that he was a bit too strong for that. "Last autumn was when your BFF screwed everything and—"

Jasmine swatted him with a folded newspaper. "Mr. Evolet Whyte, I have told you exactly one hundred thirty-nine times since the incident that if you mentioned it again you were going on my proscription list."

"I'm not on it already?" Evolet asked weakly. "Uncle Jason, doesn't that beat the Dutch?"

"It does that," Jason agreed, his eyes twinkling. "Anyway, back to what I was saying—"

"You should've been at the graduation," Jasmine remarked.

"Yes, I should've, and then our dear little Evy wouldn't be coming home with a—bandage." Jason shook his head regretfully.

"What were you going to say, Uncle Jason?" Evolet asked tactfully, as he not-so-tactfully glared daggers at his younger sister, who swatted him again.

"Well, he's a famous African criminal, but he disappeared last autumn, and has apparently reappeared here. The entire United States police force—and the FBI—are on the lookout for him. And there are rumors that if things accelerate, your parents are going to be asked to help," he added, and stood up to put his now-empty plate in the sink.

"Where do you get your information?" Evolet muttered doubtfully, but his uncle was already walking away. The younger man sighed and pushed some green beans to the corner of his plate with his fork.

"Got it," Jasmine declared suddenly, pocketing her phone. Her face wore a satisfied smirk.

Evolet suddenly paled. "You what?"

"Got an absolutely beautiful picture for Mom," his eighteen-year-old sister elaborated, pushing her chair out and standing up suddenly before he could grab her phone.

"Delete it!"

six

Hours later, while Evolet, Jasmine, and Jason ate dinner, the police searched the city for Ayan and his leopard. They took various routes in teams of four—looking for someone like Ayan, who'd evaded the African police for four years now, was extremely dangerous. The policemen knew it and were armed with doses of Schwann2, which for years now had been a part of the typical American East Coast policeman's gear. They were ready to deal with a crisis like this, or so they thought.

But a certain group of four did not notice the two dark forms huddling in the shadows behind a grocery store—until the leopard pounced.

Before they realized it, three of the men were permanently out of commission, and the fourth was on the concrete. Ayan's flashlight blinded the policeman who stared at him in horror.

A maniacal gleam in his eyes, the criminal shoved the terrified victim up against the brick wall.

"I have questions," he hissed, "and I want them answers. See?"

"Yes," the man choked out.

"So then. You heard of some Louis Stamp?" Ayan demanded, wondering if he had the name right.

"L—Louis Stamp?" the other stammered.

"I forget," Ayan growled. "Stamp, Stampon, Stanton—no, Staunton. Staunton! Louis Staunton! You hear of him?"

"I—"

"Yes, you do, no?" Ayan grinned fiendishly. "Where he be?"

The policeman wasn't about to say no to a lunatic. Taking a deep breath, he proceeded to answer Ayan's questions, and all of them.

However, unluckily for him, the policeman wasn't a complete fool, and by the time Ayan was satisfied, the cop had come up with a desperate plan to turn the tables.

So when Ayan turned around briefly to look for something, the policeman pulled out his dart gun and shot him. In the neck.

Ayan stood still.

The cop started to breathe a sigh of relief—and then froze in turn as Ayan suddenly reached his hand up to brush the dart off the back of his neck. Grabbing and inspecting it, the African wheeled around and fixed the policeman with a curious stare.

"Was this supposed to do something?" he demanded of the petrified officer.

* * *

Five minutes later, Ayan was on his way with Giza and a collection of the policemen's weapons. Discovering that more officers were on his trail, he took to the rooftops, while muttering to himself in French.

"I'm going to find that Louis Staunton." His French grammar was nothing like his bad English. "He'll help me get rid of those Whytes. He hates Evolet, too. And he's superhuman."

Giza growled in agreement, and Ayan smiled maniacally. "And now I know where he is!"

* * *

A week later, Ayan and his leopard had disappeared into thin air, much to the relief of the Cambridge population, though it was still disconcerting that the police hadn't captured the maniac.

Jasmine and Evolet had planned to go home to Annapolis for the summer, and they did so, perhaps breathing sighs of relief that the man with the wildcat didn't seem to be after them anymore. Jason came with them, and the Whytes had an enjoyable family reunion, with Alison returning from Nebraska a few days after Evolet and Jasmine.

But after three or four days of busy family life, Evolet and Jasmine wanted to get a breather, so they took to their favorite haunt: the rooftops.

They were absorbed in talking about what they called the "old days"—the end of 2041, before all the excitement with Louis and then Zaire. Evolet maintained that the trouble with Louis had really begun back in 2024, with the Purple Blitzkrieg—the brief assault of Lyndon Arnnu, their grandfather, on the United States. Jasmine agreed that her brother was right, in a way, though she was talking more about recent developments. If six years counted as recent.

"You know, it's kind of weird to think that we probably wouldn't know Uncle Jason, Uncle Petyr, and Aunt Flynn, if it weren't for Zaire," she was saying. "I can't imagine life without Uncle Jason now."

Evolet nodded. "Yeah, he's a great uncle," he agreed. "Even if he was a bad guy once."

"And a street kid," Jasmine laughed.

Evolet glared. "Okay, well, that one is not his fault."

"Wonder what it's like to be a street kid," his sister mused.

The twenty-year-old stood up and balanced near the edge of the roof, staring down at the street at least ten stories below.

"Well, I can't tell you, because I don't see any," he reported after a few seconds of glancing around. It would have made anyone dizzy, but not him.

"That's not what I meant," Jasmine muttered. "Get away from the edge or you'll fall off."

"I don't fall off," Evolet reminded her indignantly. "You're the one who likes to do that."

"Still, don't." Jasmine shut her eyes and leaned back farther on the roof. "It's stupid."

Evolet was too busy straining his eyes to pay attention to her. "The view is really great up here," he noted aloud, more to himself than to his sister. "I see...cars."

"Well, duh!" Jasmine shook her head in despair.

"And people," Evolet added quickly.

"Mhmm," Jasmine groaned.

Evolet squinted. "I don't know anyone down there, though. Oh, wait a minute, who—what—" He broke off suddenly.

"Who what what?" Jasmine questioned without opening her eyes. "I dunno, you tell me."

"Leopard," Evolet replied a moment later, taking off across the rooftop at a run.

Jasmine's eyes flew open just in time to see her brother make a crazy leap to the next rooftop.

"Leopard? Wait up!"

"Hurry up yourself!" Evolet shouted back as she began to follow him.

He kept up the running-and-jumping method, chasing the leopard. Gradually the roofs got lower, and Evolet grabbed a telephone pole and slid down it. Stepping away, he jumped up the front steps of a building, trying to get somewhere he could find the wildcat again.

Emitting a quiet *whee,* Jasmine followed him down and was at her brother's side a moment later.

"Where is it?" she demanded.

He was shading his eyes against the morning sunlight. "I dunno, I can't see him anymore," he muttered. "But I know I saw him."

"Let's walk, then," Jasmine suggested. "Maybe the police picked him up."

Evolet managed a laugh. "There'd still be a huge fight going on if they tried."

"Good point," Jasmine had to admit. "So let's go find it—him. And get this taken care of."

"Why is Ayan in Annapolis?" Evolet murmured to himself.

He darted after Jasmine as she followed her own suggestion and melted into the crowd.

seven

The two Whytes found the wildcat a couple of streets away—an area that had suddenly been deserted. Evolet and Jasmine didn't get close to the big cat, but simply peered at it discreetly from around a corner.

Jasmine pulled out her phone to get the police, just in case someone hadn't already. But the leopard was alone—or so it seemed.

"He's looking for someone," Evolet murmured to his sister, keeping his eyes on the cat.

She nodded distractedly.

Evolet was sure that the leopard couldn't hear him from that distance and over the background noise, but then the cat stopped pacing and held its nose in the air as it sniffed. Evolet tensed.

"My leopard, Giza, he sniff, he smell—superhumans."

And then, as if the leopard could sense what Evolet was thinking, it turned suddenly—and saw them.

Evolet braced himself—but he wasn't prepared for the leopard to lope off after staring at the two humans with its jaw hanging open.

Evolet's eyes widened incredulously.

"It's leaving," he whispered to Jasmine.

She had been looking at her phone, but now she glanced up in surprise. "What?"

"The cat left," Evolet repeated, looking around. "I wonder—"

And the next moment, someone dropped onto him from the overhanging roof.

Evolet yelled, jumping away as he heard the *whoosh* from above. The person smashed onto the pavement with a howl.

The two siblings backed away quickly, Jasmine having just messaged the police, and Evolet staring at the newcomer with a feeling of déjà-vu.

He had the weirdest, creepiest feeling he'd seen the person before—this man who picked himself up gingerly and turned to glare at Evolet out of crazy gray eyes.

His jaw was hard. He was tall, with dark brown hair, and dressed in dark clothes. And he looked straight at Evolet, his eyes burning.

Evolet was totally confused until the man spoke one sentence.

"I told you I would kill you too."

"Creep," Evolet muttered to himself as the memories flooded back to him. "Blast!"

"Who?" Jasmine squinted.

"Staunton," Evolet shouted to her as he jumped away from the incoming Louis. "Call the cops this time, will you!"

"They're already coming," she retorted, stuffing her phone into her pocket where hopefully it wouldn't get broken. She circled around Louis so that he was between her and Evolet.

They knew that Louis had been in an asylum for the past five years. What was he doing here?

Neither Evolet nor Jasmine could tell how he'd gotten out, for the life of them. But they knew the man neeed to be contained. ASAP.

The Whyte siblings braced themselves for a fight.

But now Louis did more than threaten. Bursting into insane laughter, he pulled out a handgun and aimed it directly at Evolet.

It took half an instant for Evolet to register the motion, and then another for him to drop as Louis pulled the trigger.

He rolled forward into Louis, barely avoiding the shots that followed.

Louis was completely overwhelmed in the next few seconds, when Jasmine pounced like a cat from behind just as Evolet—curled into a ball—slammed into the maniac's legs.

The next moment, Louis found himself sitting hard on the ground, the younger of his captors aiming his own gun at him, and the other staring at him very seriously.

"You have the right to remain silent," Evolet told their prisoner gravely as Jasmine tapped away on her phone. "Or maybe not. Whichever you prefer."

He took a quick step back as Louis spat at him. "I told you I would kill you. You'll see. You. Conner. And—" his face twisted as he glared with hate at Jasmine "—that girl."

Evolet shook his head. "That's not going to help your case—"

"We will kill you, I tell you," Louis went on obliviously. "We will. So watch your back, and watch for knives, and—"

"Who is *we?*" Jasmine asked suddenly. All the talk of murder wasn't scaring her, but the word *we* made her reconsider the danger.

"We" meant this lunatic, and who else?

Suddenly silent, Louis grinned.

"Who is *we?*" Evolet repeated after his sister, glancing keenly at Louis. He, too, was interested. And just a bit surprised. Had Louis teamed up with someone?

"*We* am we!" came a new voice from behind him, and Evolet jumped.

Jasmine flinched, and Louis took that moment to knock the gun out of her hand and spring to his feet.

The two Whytes turned around to see Giza and Ayan leaping at them.

"Oh heavens," Evolet gasped, spinning around before the two newcomers got there to kick Louis away from them both.

Jasmine tackled Ayan, but Giza sprang directly onto Evolet's shoulders.

Evolet screamed, the wildcat breathing down his neck, and fell over backwards on top of it before he realized he wasn't actually being clawed; his mother's old jacket protected him.

The cat yowled and jumped out from underneath him, the claws reaching for his face.

Squeezing his eyes shut tight, Evolet yelled for help while he folded his legs underneath the leopard and then straightened them, sending the wildcat flying off him and straight into Louis.

"Jasmine, where are the cops!" he yelled distractedly as he spun out of

Giza's returning path and landed on his feet just in time to swing around a lamppost and kick Louis away again, in the face this time.

Jasmine was busy giving Ayan a cooking lesson: how to very sportsman-likely provide one's opponent with knuckle sandwiches. "On the way, I said!" she shouted back, also somewhat distractedly.

"Oh," Evolet muttered as he began to hear the first wails of an approaching siren. He smiled grimly, stepping aside as Louis ran towards him, flailing his fists.

But after fighting the untrained Ayan the other day, and mostly amateur fighters in the past five years, Evolet wasn't prepared for Louis to put his Violet Army experience into use and kick his legs from under him.

He rolled away before Louis could do more damage, however. Evolet glanced towards Jasmine, only to open his mouth for a horrified shriek.

"Behind you!"

The warning came just in time. Jasmine gave Ayan a final punch that blew him off his feet, and spun around to face the leopard flying towards her. Apparently the cat had given up on Evolet.

Jasmine stared in shock for a moment, and then she did the only thing she could think of. She grabbed Ayan and shoved him directly into the leopard's path.

Ayan let out a bloodcurdling scream. It mingled with the police sirens as the professionals arrived on the scene.

Louis stared at his friend Ayan as Evolet and Jasmine backed away, letting the policemen take charge of the situation.

Evolet glanced at his sister worriedly.

"Are you okay?" he demanded. "I thought the cat was about to land on your back."

"I'm fine," she told him, but he noticed a small cut on her lip.

"You're sure?"

"Oh, hang it, Evy, I'm fine!" she gritted, watching Louis as he bent over to Ayan, who was on the ground. The police surrounded them carefully, guns at the ready.

Then Ayan got up and the three attackers crashed away, knocking policemen over in their wake.

Evolet and Jasmine stared, too exhausted to do anything about it, and then sighed. Why did superhumans seem to be the only ones who could deal with superhumans?

Evolet saw a policeman heading over to them—two, in fact. He groaned.

"Blast!"

eight

"Stupid college, stupid America, stupid too smart kids!" Ayan was fuming hours later. He, Louis, and Giza had lost the police and eventually found their way to their current hideout: an old, run-down building near the Annapolis waterfront.

They were having dinner, if "dinner" included half-cooked fish that would have sickened anyone but maniacs. Ayan wasn't really eating his; he was pacing, muttering incessantly. But Louis seemed to have more sense, and he made sure to eat something, even if Giza wolfed down most of their catch.

"Is stupid your favorite word?" Louis wondered, glancing hard at his roommate.

Ayan's coral eyes narrowed into slits. "Stupid English!"

"Do you speak something else?" Louis asked.

"French, nothing," Ayan returned, calming down somewhat.

Apparently the two had some connection that enabled them to hold a conversation without trying to kill each other. Perhaps it was because both men were well and truly insane.

Louis ignored the response and stood up as well, glancing around the room.

"I was going to kill Trooper here," he announced officiously. "I almost did."

"Why not?" Ayan glared.

"Because that boy of his—Evolet—stopped me. But Trooper ruined everything. And his friends killed my sister. I will kill Trooper," Louis muttered. "I will kill him!"

"We kill him," Ayan insisted. "Him and Evolet and Jasmine and them all."

"But how?" Louis murmured, and then suddenly fixed his gaze on Ayan. "I cannot alone. *We* cannot alone. We proved that today. How will we do it?"

"We need more cats," Ayan decided after a moment's thought. "Big cats." He stroked Giza's fur appreciatively, as if he'd already forgotten that Giza had given him a new scar that day.

"No." Louis shook his head, but his eyes lit up suddenly. "Not cats. Superhumans. Superhumans do not attack comrades."

Ayan squinted. "What that means?"

"That means, we need people," Louis explained, gaining momentum as he warmed to his idea. "If we kidnap people, then we can give them T4, and make them work for us." His eyes flashed.

"They work for us, just like that?" Ayan frowned.

Louis shook his head pityingly. "No, we'll have to make them. Giza is scary, he'll help with that. He can help with the injections, too, seeing as we don't have a laboratory." He frowned. "We ought to."

"You mean how he gave me injection thing," Ayan realized suddenly. "Yes, that work! And then we have army."

"Yes! We'll beat them for sure, then." Suddenly Louis frowned. "Do we kidnap adults or children?"

"Children no fight," Ayan returned. "Adults."

"But adults won't want to fight," Louis mused. "Not that children will, but we can make them do it more easily." He snapped his fingers. "If we use children, that's even better! I know Trooper, I know the Whytes. They won't fight children."

"Then we win!" Ayan shouted triumphantly.

Louis rubbed his hands together. "Yeah, we'll win!"

He grinned to himself. "We'll start tonight."

* * *

"Conner, Violet, we need your help. We apologize for not telling you first about Louis Staunton's escape. But there are things to be done. We'll tell you everything we know about it."

Conner shook his head slowly, glancing at Violet. She was doing some laundry at the other end of the garage. Conner had been just about to head over to the police station to find out what was going on. But then the police themselves had called him.

He cleared his throat. "Okay—for now. I already heard the entire story from the kids' point of view. What do you have?"

"The escape report from the asylum, various witnesses's stories of other attacks, and, most relevantly, details concerning a kidnapping. Joyce Liszt is already on it. What do you say?"

Conner glanced at Violet again. He knew she was listening—she always was when she was nearby—and she nodded in confirmation.

"We're in," Conner told the officer. "Fire away."

"Okay. First of all, Louis Staunton has escaped the asylum. He had help from Ayan Monet."

Conner nodded. "Mhmm."

"They've been loose together for the last three days. Some people have seen them with the wildcat. And then, yesterday afternoon, your children were targeted."

"Right. Go on," Conner urged, waiting to learn something new.

"Well, late last night, they kidnapped a couple of kids and murdered the parents. The camera footage makes their identities clear. And they've taken the two kids and disappeared."

Conner tensed, frowning.

Murder and kidnapping?

"Why would they do that?"

"If only we knew," the officer muttered. "Anyway. We haven't been able to find them. Joyce Liszt has been on the case since Staunton escaped. But now that it's obvious that Staunton and Monet have teamed up, and that they are up to something other than—err—"

Something other than attacking the Whytes, was that it?

"I get it," Conner interrupted, his voice suddenly cold. "Joyce needs our help."

"Exactly," the man went on, obviously relieved. Perhaps Conner's sarcasm hadn't gotten through the phone. "You got the amber alert late last evening? Well, there's going to be another alert in a few minutes, once I get off this phone call. Annapolis is going under lockdown. Of course, the lockdown doesn't apply to you or your family."

Conner smiled slightly. "Okay."

"Thanks. And one last thing—can you meet Liszt at *Pervitto's* downtown in half an hour?"

"I guess," Conner shrugged.

"Good. She'll fill you in."

Conner hung up and glanced at his wife.

She shook her head. "Here we go again."

nine

"Their summer rental house had an automatic 9-1-1 dialing mechanism," Joyce was telling Conner and Violet over a plateful of Alfredo pasta, about thirty minutes later. "That's how we knew about it almost right away. They shot the parents—they've been collecting weapons from police patrols, it seems—and took the two kids: Michael and Dawn Leblanc, here in Annapolis for vacation. Michael is twelve, and Dawn is—"

"Three," Violet interrupted. "They're the kids Evolet, Jasmine, and Jason helped last autumn, right?"

Joyce smiled grimly. "Actually, she's four now, but yes. It's probably just a coincidence that they're the same children, but that's the fact. Anyway, Staunton and Monet have disappeared with the two—and their leopard—and we have no idea where to start looking, except here in Annapolis, because the two seemed to be targeting you guys. That is, until last night."

"If they're targeting us, why didn't we get told?" Conner frowned.

Their friend, the only civilian-accepted superhuman besides the Whytes, shrugged uneasily. "I'm not quite sure why, but I think the general reason is that it'd be easier to track Louis and Ayan down if you were unaware. And you Whytes are quite capable of taking care of yourselves, as recent events have proved. But now we need help."

She winced. "As you heard, after today everything will be closed down in Annapolis, until either Staunton and Monet leave, or they're dealt with. The police will cooperate with us, but as of now, it's the three of us who are going to be doing the main work."

Violet nodded slowly, but Conner was still somewhat distrustful. If Evolet and Jasmine hadn't been, well, themselves, then yesterday's events could have ended far more badly.

"And we have a promise that we're going to be updated on anything and everything, from now on?" he asked Joyce.

The paratrooper nodded. "That's correct."

Conner and Violet looked at each other, and nodded together. "Let's get going."

* * *

That night, Annapolis went into lockdown. Most of the civilians were terrified; they made sure to lock every window and door securely. They'd only been told that dangerous superhumans were on the loose and that they were in danger if they went outside or anything of the sort from now on. The police would take care of food supplies and other necessities until the crisis was over. They would also be patrolling the city at every hour of the day and night.

But that did not prevent eleven more children, between the ages of eight and fourteen, from being kidnapped during the night, all from different families—it seemed that the night before had been a mere experiment. Again the story was the same, except this time it was only Louis and the leopard who finished the parents and disappeared with the children.

But as dawn broke over Annapolis, the quietest dawn the city had ever seen, Conner, Violet, Joyce, and a SWAT team were closing in.

Or so they thought.

The three superhumans had arrived on the scene of the last kidnapping only minutes after the perpetrator and victim vanished. The three followed the killers to an old and disused windowless warehouse. Joyce phoned the police, while Conner and Violet kept watch to make sure no one left the building.

Then, with the police, they broke into the building—only to discover that the power was out. They stopped short just inside the door, each one fumbling for a flashlight.

Then the hair on the back of Conner's neck rose as his super-keen ears became aware of a low and barely distinguishable growl.

He lifted his light just in time to see Ayan's big cat leaping at him.

Without a moment's hesitation, he pulled his gun off his belt and shot at it, once, twice, thrice—until he ran out of ammunition.

The leopard landed on him nonetheless, but then the cat's claws dug into his face, and Conner fell backwards from the weight. The cat began to go limp.

Giza yowled, and then Conner easily shoved him off after Violet emptied her own gun into the wildcat.

Conner stood up, panting as he touched his face lightly and cringed. He was bleeding from four deep cuts across his left cheek.

"I—I think that finished it," he murmured, prodding the cat tentatively with his booted foot. It didn't move, and he breathed a sigh of relief, trying not to look at the mess it was after about twenty rounds had been shot into it.

"Good," Violet returned absentmindedly, pulling off her jacket. She tossed it to her husband while the police and Joyce rushed ahead of them to investigate the rest of the building. "You'd better clean those cuts before they get infected."

Conner laughed ironically. "If they're going to get infected, they already are," he muttered. "That cat was literally drooling on my face. Not like I'd get sick, anyway."

He caught his wife's jacket and looked at it, shaking his head. "I'm not getting blood on this."

"Yes you are," Violet retorted. She'd started to follow the others, but now she turned around to glance at Conner. "It'll wash out."

"Fine," he sighed, but he wasn't so reluctant to clean his face off that he protested further. He let the others go on, holding Violet's trademark purple jacket to his face and taking deep breaths as he waited for the T4 to do its work and patch him up.

Usually he would have stopped bleeding almost right away. Conner frowned annoyedly as it continued to hurt.

He had some deep cuts, but the T4 should have dulled the sting by now.

"Maybe I'm getting old," he muttered. "Forty-five? Is that old?"

And then he caught his breath as his cheek, and then his face, and then suddenly his entire body, started to burn like fire.

He wanted to scream, but instead, he clenched his free hand into a tight fist.

The pain didn't go away. What was going on?

Conner hadn't felt real pain in over twenty years.

And never anything like this.

He stood there, not moving for fear it would accelerate something.

After what seemed like hours, the others returned with their flashlights.

"No one else here," Joyce began disappointedly. "Louis must've gotten away with the child—Conner, what's wrong?" she interrupted herself suddenly, staring at his white face.

He shook his head dizzily. "I don't know."

Violet stepped over to him and gently took her jacket away from his face. She started.

"Something is reacting with your T4. You're scarring. And purple."

ten

"They killed Giza," Ayan mourned. "You stupid!" he yelled savagely at Louis. "You leave him there be shoot!"

"At least we got the kids," Louis shot back, only slightly perturbed. He glanced around him at the crowd of thirteen children, all of whom seemed petrified at the yelling contest between their two captors. "And now I bet we have enough. We can finish now. If we need more, then we can get more. Simple!"

Ayan growled, resentful. "He good, tame cat."

"Leopards can't be tamed," Louis glared.

"You leave him there be shoot," Ayan snapped stubbornly.

He was in a world of his own now, as he sat cross-legged against the wall and tapped the floor annoyedly.

Louis decided to ignore him, and he glanced around again, taking count of their new assets. "Eleven. Twelve. Thirteen!"

They stared back at him in mute fright.

Louis smiled maniacally, which did not help matters. "Since we don't have the cat anymore, we'll have to do this another way," he mused, jumping up and going to a corner of the room. He felt around in a box and and pulled out some medical supplies, including a syringe filled with a dark red liquid.

Suddenly Ayan was at his side. "What you doing?" he hissed.

"Giving them the injection," Louis retorted calmly, brushing him aside.

"You say we have no lab!" Ayan flared. "You lie!"

"Yes, but then I went to a lab and got this stuff. For free," Louis added ominously, advancing towards the first of the children, an eight-year-old boy, who shrank against the wall in terror.

From the other end of the room, Michael Leblanc watched, four-year-old Dawn asleep on his lap. He had his hand on her forehead.

She was so hot. Like she'd been during the fever that had made her go deaf a year ago. Except she could hear now.

Michael knew this was no fever. Because he had it, too.

It had to be the same thing as the injection Louis was giving the newer children now, he decided as the boy Louis was injecting began to scream.

An hour or so after he and Dawn had been kidnapped, they'd been brought here.

Then Ayan had told his leopard to attack Michael. Though the man had waited only a few seconds before calling the cat off, Michael's face and right arm had been deeply scored. The boy had been screaming then. Bloodstains still marked the wooden floor.

But the pain from that was nothing compared to what came afterward. Michael would have tried to stop them doing the same thing to Dawn. But his blood had begun to burn, incessantly, horribly, unstoppably. He had felt himself becoming superhumanly strong, but he felt the pain more.

And even when the cuts stopped bleeding and scarred purple like Ayan's, it still hurt. Even now it hurt. He felt it would drive him mad.

But he wasn't going to let it, he told himself, looking down at his sister. He didn't want to see the other kids anymore. He knew what they were going through, though they weren't getting scarred in the process. Michael fought the mixed feelings of despair and power that flooded him and looked down at his younger sister. He couldn't give in to the pain. He had to stay strong—for Dawn.

There was one thing the injection had done for her, he knew. She could hear now. She had heard him earlier that day. It had been wonderful. But he knew there was another change, though he didn't want to believe it. She wasn't herself. Maybe she was frightened. But she wasn't Dawn.

It scared him that his sister would act and talk like that, as if she were insane. He tried to tell himself that she was just too worried and tired and sad to think right. But deep down, he knew. She'd given in to the injection—like he suspected Ayan had done. She hadn't fought it like Michael still was. She really was insane—if such a word could apply to a four-year-old. Michael hoped desperately that there was a way to make it stop.

He shut his eyes tightly, remembering their kidnapping. It had been so sudden. One minute they were all having dinner together, and the next, their parents were on the ground and the two kids were screaming. It had been a nightmare.

He clenched his fists.

Michael would not give in. He would stay himself.

He would protect Dawn, and they would survive together, no matter how their captors planned to use them. And there was one thing the injection had done for them: it had given them a better chance at survival.

Thinking of the word "superhuman," he remembered the three people who had rescued them last autumn: Jason Foley, Evolet Whyte, and Jasmine Whyte. He wondered if this was the same sort of thing—and, if so, was he stronger or weaker than they were?

He had no idea how soon he was going to find out.

Nor how.

* * *

It was a few days before Conner was back to his normal self. Meanwhile, Joyce kept searching with the police while Violet ran tests to find out what was Conner's problem, exactly. Though she didn't get results until he was completely better, she discovered something so important she told him anyway.

"That thing the leopard had, it wasn't T4," she told him as they drove off to find Joyce. "It was a sort of combination of T4 and T5. So—T6."

"T6?" Conner frowned. "And he gave it to me?"

"Yes, but if you've stopped hurting, then I think your T4 has gotten rid of it," she explained. "I'm not too good on the technical details, but the person I sent the results to—Eternyti Schwann, she's a smart scientist—told me that basically, with T6, T4 and T5 are combating each other, and neither can win. So the person with T6 has a perpetual fever, and, like you had, a burning feeling—well, everywhere. Everywhere there is blood, meaning, blood with T4 and T5. So—everywhere," she finished awkwardly.

"So you're saying that I had T5 in me for a few days," Conner mused slowly. "Not enough to turn my hair white and my eyes coral, thankfully, like your relatives—but enough to fight T4."

"Exactly," Violet nodded emphatically. "That's exactly it."

"At least it's gone now," Conner murmured.

"That's not all, though," Violet went on. "I have a theory now about Ayan Monet. It's only a theory, but—"

"Well, fire away," Conner grinned.

Violet closed her eyes. "What if the leopard gave it to Monet? As we've seen, Monet has very obviously been in fights with that cat before. His scars are proof of that. But where else could Monet have gotten it?"

"I think the question is, how did the leopard get it?" Conner furrowed his brows. "Monet could have gotten it first and given it to the leopard, I suppose. But how did T4 and T5 combined get to Africa—"

He cut short. Violet's mouth dropped open.

"Zaire," she breathed. "He went to Africa."

Conner nodded slowly. "It must have been him. But I thought he just had T5. Hyper-T5, I mean."

Violet tilted her head thoughtfully. "I dunno, but he must've gotten a potent dose of T4 for it to turn into T6. And then I guess the leopard got it from him and gave it to Monet about a year later, seeing as Monet's been active in Africa for only four years and it's been five since Zaire was taken care of. Yes? No?"

"Makes sense to me," Conner agreed, frowning. "But where did Zaire get T4?"

He was slightly surprised the next moment as Violet tensed visibly.

"I wonder," she whispered, more to herself than to him.

"Huh?" Conner didn't hear her.

"I don't know for sure," Violet told him, louder this time.

He glanced sideways at her for a moment before turning his attention back to the road.

Conner had thought his wife's reticence had disappeared in the last five years. But here it was again, just as strong as when they'd been fighting Louis.

Or maybe it was because they'd been fighting Louis, and that would explain it now.

Except she hadn't know they were fighting Louis back then.

Or had she?

eleven

ichael was shocked to discover that the Whyte family was the two maniacs' target. He found that out about five days after he and Dawn had been kidnapped, a day before the others.

The two adults had decided to keep the children's number at thirteen, and so they hadn't kidnapped any more. But at this point Michael was horrified to see that most of the others were losing their sanity as well. Only he and three others were still fighting to stay in reality.

But they weren't allowed to talk together much. Louis made sure of that. He seemed to be much more intelligent than Ayan—his obsession with killing the Whytes was the main reason he was insane.

Michael found that out by listening to their conversation, when Ayan started complaining about the "fire" one evening and Louis brought up his own story.

They were talking together quietly, probably confident that the children were too tired and hurting to care what they were saying, but Michael cared. Especially when he heard the name "Evolet."

"Evolet, Jasmine, that Jason Foley person, and then Conner and Violet, of course. If we can lay a trap for all five of them, using the kids, we can finish them off then. It's good we have the kids; they'll make good bait. But it has to be a very good trap. And Violet might even join us. We used to work together," Louis added vehemently. "And she is an amazing fighter."

"She fight with us, good then," Ayan laughed. "But how we do trap?"

"I've been thinking about it for the past few days," Louis told him confidently. "We need to take the kids somewhere else, and train them—

they'll be no good without training, unless we use them as hostages. But if we can make them obey us, that's even better. And if we take them somewhere else it'll be hard for Conner and the others to find us—until we're ready. Then they'll find us alright." His mouth curved into an insane smirk.

"Well, where we go then?" Ayan asked impatiently. "No need stupid long explain."

Louis's eyes narrowed into slits, but he ignored the insult. "We can go to Nevada. There are lots of mountains there, and we can find one far away from cities and set up camp there for a couple of weeks. And then we can set our trap." He grinned.

Ayan sprang to his feet. "When leave?" he demanded eagerly.

"No, not now, you idiot!" Louis hissed. "Wait till it's dark. We can leave then." He glanced at all the kids thoughtfully and turned to Ayan. "Can you drive?"

* * *

"It definitely looks as if they've evacuated," Joyce declared mournfully to Conner over the phone the next morning. "A van was stolen. We inspected the buildings nearby and found traces of Louis, Ayan, and the kids. But they've left the building—if not the city."

Conner sighed. "When will we know if they've left Annapolis?"

"We're looking into that right now," Joyce assured him. "We'll probably know within a couple of days. But the chief asked me to let you know that you can take a break for now. I'll let you know when things start up again. We have to find those kids and deal with Monet and Staunton."

"Yes, we do," Conner agreed emphatically. "So you want Violet and me to stay out of your way for the next day or so."

Joyce laughed. "Yeah, that's about it. But the chief didn't say you have to follow the lockdown, either—"

"It's fine," Conner broke in. "I was joking anyway. But I guess we'll see you soon."

"See you," Joyce returned, hanging up.

Conner put his phone down on the table and glanced over at Violet. "We have a few days' break."

"Good," she grinned. "Because Jason just told me that Petyr and Flynn are coming for a visit. They'll be here for a few weeks."

"Two more people," Conner sighed. "Where are we going to put everyone?" Nowadays, he, Violet, his sister Moira, and his son Charles lived in the house Conner and Moira had grown up in. Right now, it was quite snug, with Jason, Evolet, Jasmine, and Alison there as well.

Violet shrugged. "Maybe they'll stay at a hotel."

"Maybe," Conner acquiesced doubtfully. After a moment's thought, he smiled. "I just hope we don't have more family members popping up anytime soon. Got any more jacks-in-the-box?"

"I think that was all," she returned gravely, though her eyes twinkled. "No need to worry."

"Good." Conner set his jaw firmly. "Quite enough kidnappings in our families."

Violet's eyebrows shot up. "Is that supposed to have some kind of implication?"

* * *

Eternyti Schwann, as Violet had introduced her, was indeed a very smart scientist—a sort of genius. Twenty-five-years-old, she was somewhat young to have her own laboratory in Texas, but she did: Eternity Labs.

It was in a nice, unpopulated, desert-like area with plenty of room to expand. There, she and her scientists worked on their projects, mostly pertaining to the environment. At this point, Eternyti was so well set up that all she usually had to do was issue instructions. But lately she'd gotten a project she was excited to work on herself.

Normally, an enterprising scientist like her wouldn't have gotten their hands on T4, T5, or T6. That sort of stuff was kept locked up in government laboratories and in secure storage. But Violet Whyte, who trusted her friends more than she trusted the government—understandably—had sent her a sample of Conner's blood to analyze.

But even after Eternyti sent her test results back, she hadn't stopped. She kept experimenting. She had access to Schwann2—that was common stuff, since it could only be used to harm superhumans—and she tried to see if it would work, after she separated T4, T5, HT5, and T6 from the blood sample. As she'd expected, Schwann2 only worked on T4 and T5.

But she wasn't looking for a toxin for HT5 and T6 now; she was looking for a cure. So, working with Schwann2, she set out to find that cure.

Eternyti liked to say that if there was an evil, there was a good—a cure for the evil. So she took that literally in this case, looking for the cure to the "evil," as she supposed it to be.

And rightly, too. Ever since T4 had been invented, superhumans—or would-be superhumans—had been causing trouble. Eternyti might have liked to be a superhuman herself, but she also liked to stick to the law, and it was a felony to willfully inject oneself with T4.

But since she couldn't be, and more especially because of her own personal thoughts on the matter, she decided she was going to find a way to undo the work of the injection. She knew the government would be approve of *that*.

Superhumans were dangerous. They should be gotten rid of, or at least suppressed. And Eternyti was going to do that. Especially now that she'd heard about what was going on in Annapolis. The city was the most chaotic it had been since the Purple Blitzkrieg.

It was all because of T4 and T6. But Eternyti was going to change that.

twelve

I t was two weeks before the Whyte adults heard anything more about what was going on.

Meanwhile, Evolet and Jasmine were getting extremely annoyed that they weren't being allowed to do anything to help out. Not to mention their uncle—Jason should have been contacted. But he was still on probation from what had happened five years before, it seemed, and the police wanted him staying out of it.

And Conner and Violet wanted Evolet and Jasmine to stay safe, especially after they'd nearly been killed when they were attacked by Ayan, Louis, and the leopard. But now Conner, Violet, and Joyce were heading to Nevada to deal with a report of Louis and Ayan being there, and Evolet, Jasmine, and Jason were chaffing to follow.

"It's completely not fair," Evolet complained for the hundredth time that summer to his sister and uncle. "We're all adults here. It's Jasmine and me that those guys are after, if we exclude Dad. Mom and Dad get asked by the government to handle this, but we have to stay home. It's not fair!"

"Life isn't fair," Jason remarked. He sighed.

"It should be," Jasmine muttered.

They were on a rooftop somewhere in Annapolis. When weren't they, when something important was going on?

Though the two had invited Jason to come with them this time. Because Evolet had a plan.

"If you didn't notice, Uncle Jason," he began, not hesitating at all as Jason was now completely part of the family, "Mom and Dad didn't really, strictly, order us to stay home. And everyone is ignoring you.”

Jason glanced up at him from where he was idly inspecting a lightning rod. “Meaning?”

“Meaning we could just follow them to Nevada,” Jasmine put in, winking at Evolet behind Jason’s back.

“Ha,” Jason laughed. He turned so that neither of them could see his face. “There’s a lockdown.”

“That doesn’t apply to us, Dad said.” Evolet frowned. “What if Aunt Moira is okay with it?” he suggested quietly after a moment or two. “I bet we can get her to agree,” he added hurriedly as Jasmine’s eyebrows shot up.

“By means of torture, or what?” she asked thoughtfully.

He scowled. “By asking, of course! Uncle Jason, would you come with us? She’s 99 percent likely to say yes if you do.” Evolet’s voice was hopeful.

“She’s 100 percent likely to say no,” Jasmine muttered. Evolet glared at her.

But finally Jason turned around, keeping an impossibly straight face. “Fine, I think I’ll come along—*if* you can get your aunt to agree that this is a good idea.”

“Oh, we will,” Evolet promised, elated.

“By fair means or foul,” Jasmine added darkly.

This time Evolet couldn’t restrain himself from growling in disgust. “Can you not do that?” he asked flatly.

“Whatever,” Jasmine mumbled, after glancing at her brother warily. “Let’s go talk to Aunt Moira, then!”

* * *

“Incredibly dumb,” was Moira’s first response.

Though she was Conner’s twin sister, she looked much older than him, as she didn’t have the youth that T4 implied. She was basically a second mother to Evolet, as she’d brought him up when Conner and Violet Whyte were in Iceland with Evolet’s younger siblings. And Moira was very adamant about his staying out of trouble.

His face fell. "But what if Mom and Dad need help?"

"Then they would've asked you to come with them," Moira insisted.

"But they didn't say we *couldn't* come," Jasmine pleaded.

"And they didn't say you *could* come, either." Moira crossed her arms. "Run off and play."

"But we're adults," Evolet protested.

Moira's eyebrows shot up. "Then why are you asking to go to Nevada like you're both six years old?"

Jasmine choked very suddenly, and Evolet flushed. "Well, I mean—"

Moira got serious. "Listen, if Jason is going with you, then I guess it's okay. Not like you need me to say yes, anyway. Your parents could well need help. But if you don't stay safe...they will kill me," she sighed.

"Oh, we'll be safe," Evolet promised, jumping at the chance. "We'll be *very* safe, I promise!"

Moira laughed, brushing his thick brown hair out of his face, one of her favorite things to do. Now she had to reach up to do it, as he was taller than she was.

"And whatever you do, don't get coral eyes like your dad did for a week. That was creepy."

"We won't. It definitely was," Jasmine agreed emphatically.

The three fell into a pensive silence.

"Well?" Moira demanded. "What are you two waiting for?"

"Nothing!"

Grinning his thanks, Evolet turned and fled before she could give them any more instructions. Chuckling, Jasmine followed as they went to find Jason.

"She's okay with it," Evolet reported breathlessly once they finally discovered their uncle in the garage looking at his car.

Jason didn't look up. "She is? Good. Then you two had better pack."

"Pack?" they echoed in surprise.

He nodded, sighing. "It'll take us over a day to get there in the car, maybe two days, so we'll need to stop at a hotel on the way. Plus, we'll be there long enough to finish this up. So yes, pack."

"Oh," Evolet breathed, registering the information. He nodded furiously and dashed off towards his old—now Charles's mostly—bedroom. Jasmine in turn went to the room she was sharing with Moira. Grabbing her suitcase off the closet shelf, she took a look at it and shook her head.

"Too big," she muttered, replacing it on the shelf and grabbing a backpack instead. It took her about ten minutes to collect all her essentials.

She put on the backpack. It would've been heavy for anyone else, but not for Jasmine Whyte. She grinned at a mirror.

"Nevada, here we come!"

thirteen

"I don't like this," Conner was muttering a few days later as he, Violet, Joyce, and FBI police began the long trek up a Nevada mountain—two days after Jason, Evolet, and Jasmine left Annapolis. "They could be anywhere around here—and we wouldn't know a thing about it in the dark. I don't like this at all."

Violet, too, seemed uneasy. Still, she kept up a carefree attitude and marched uniformly on, maneuvering her flashlight carefully to guide herself around logs, thorns, and the like. It was around eleven at night, but they were going up the mountain now because they had concrete evidence that Ayan and Louis were up there somewhere.

"Darkness gives us an element of surprise," she retorted quietly. "And besides, the mountain's surrounded. They won't be getting away."

Conner nodded, but he was still disturbed. "And we're making too much noise and showing too much light to catch them by surprise, anyway, especially as we don't even know where they are," he noted, sighing.

"These flashlights are made to only shine a certain distance. And we could be quieter if the FBI weren't along," Violet muttered, and Conner regretted what he'd said.

"Never mind." He shook his head.

"But I like the dark," Violet went on, speaking softly. "Especially night marches like this." Conner saw her almost shiver.

He wrinkled his brow in confusion. "Why on earth?"

"I don't know," she whispered back.

He shrugged. And then everyone they were with, including themselves, stopped short and went completely silent as they saw a light moving somewhere farther up the mountain.

"What is that?" Conner heard someone mutter.

And that was when he became aware of a prickling sensation.

A sixth sense—the one that told him someone was watching him.

He froze—so did Violet and Joyce. Then Conner recovered himself and wheeled around, shining his flashlight into the darkness. It only pierced the black night a few feet before it melted away.

But he knew someone was there, or somewhere around there.

And then he got the cold feeling again, and turned around once more. Still nothing. But his T4 had given him an amplified sixth sense.

"We're surrounded," he murmured to Violet. "Spread the word."

As events turned out, she didn't have to. The next moment, someone started firing from the trees at the policemen. With his keen sense of hearing, Conner could tell that there were at least three separate shooters.

"What on earth?" he spluttered, but no one heard him over the confused shouts of the policemen, as well as the sudden and short-lived screams. Conner and Violet raised their own guns at the same time and began shooting back. Joyce was doing the same thing, as were a few policeman who were quicker on the uptake as the others.

Then a child's scream rent the air, and Conner's blood ran cold.

"Oh heavens, no," he whispered, breaking out in cold sweat. Ayan and Louis were using the children!

"STOP! Everybody stop!" Violet screamed desperately, having realized the same thing.

Everyone with them stopped firing, but the people in the trees didn't. But there were only two of them now, Violet realized with a feeling of horror.

A man's wild laughter broke out from somewhere to Conner's left, and without a moment's hesitation, he started shooting in that direction. The laughing just continued, and with a wave of frustration, Conner realized he couldn't even see what he was shooting at.

Replacing his gun in his belt with a swift, fluid movement, he ignored a bullet that grazed his arm, and charged off in the direction of the laughter.

Violet had lost her flashlight, which she figured was a good thing since the tree snipers were targeting the lights. Realizing that, the policemen disposed of their lights as well, and they were all left in utter blackness. It was then that they were suddenly attacked on all sides by people armed with guns, tasers, and dart guns.

It was an utter massacre.

Violet knew it in the first moments of the fighting that followed. Everyone was just shooting wildly, though their ambushers seemed to have picked targets.

Violet got hit in the shoulder, though she fought on, and then suddenly someone cannoned into her, shooting blindly. She fell over backwards, hit probably about six times in various places, something her T4 couldn't handle all at once. Gasping, she tried to shove her attacker off—and then realized it was a kid. A superhuman kid, who made her think of her own, and then she couldn't hurt him.

"Stop! We're your friends!" she screamed at him. Or maybe it was a her. She couldn't tell in the darkness. But he didn't listen, so she grabbed him by the shoulders very tightly and tossed him off, then fell back completely from the effort.

She thought she was going to die. Maybe she was. She was bleeding hard and getting weaker by the second.

Slowly the screams died down. Conner was shouting her name. But she didn't answer him. She was gasping so hard for breath that she didn't have enough air to waste on words.

She wonders distantly if she'd been hit in the lungs. All six shots had been in that area. Were they fatal? She didn't know; she hadn't studied first aid. But as far as she could tell, the T4 wasn't doing much, if anything.

Violet had a sinking feeling that the more blood—and T4—she lost, the less likely she would be to recover. She tried to remind herself that one didn't have to be superhuman to outlive a fight.

But now, after years of being strong and healthy, something like this was frightening.

She didn't want to die, she realized suddenly. Not now. She wasn't ready.

Gradually, she realized that everything had fallen silent, except for someone moaning somewhere. The guns were finally quiet. Then someone started talking. She strained her aching ears.

Now someone else was talking, she realized. Louis. And then Conner again. She wondered dimly what they were talking about, while she also pondered if it was possible to pass out with T4. Because she felt incredibly like passing out at the moment. Or she would've if she didn't have a feeling that Conner might need her.

How she *could* be of any help right now was another question.

Someone turned on a light. A huge floodlight that lit up the entire area. If only that had been on before. Violet's eyes took a moment to adjust, and then she could see, though from the ground.

She had been right.

They'd been fighting *kids.*

fourteen

"Up there! There's fighting up there!" Evolet shouted to his uncle and Jasmine after listening for a few seconds.

At the base of the mountain, they began running up, somehow finding their way through the darkness. They could hear guns going off, far above them—what sounded like dozens of them.

It was a wild dash up the mountainside, and at one point Jasmine slipped and began sliding down to the very bottom, but Evolet grabbed her hand just in time. It was lucky for both of them that they were superhuman.

But finally the three got to the top, Jason in the lead, just when the fighting area flooded with light.

Rubbing his eyes, Jason jumped back into the shadows before anyone could notice him and motioned to his niece and nephew to stay out of the light as well.

Evolet shook his head in dismay as his eyes adjusted to the light, allowing him to take in the scene.

It was horrifying.

There were about three kids on the ground, one of them looking about four.

His mother was on the ground as well, and so was Joyce Liszt. Conner was locked in some kind of deadly struggle with Louis and Ayan both. Evolet bit his lip, even as he began running forward to help out with his uncle and sister.

Conner was obviously putting up a final, desperate struggle, and losing it; he was breathing heavily, with blood streaming down his face and then from somewhere else around his chest.

He kept fighting doggedly, but even as Evolet, Jasmine, and Jason were running the last yards, Louis pulled out a gun and shot his opponent repeatedly. Conner crumpled to the ground, beaten.

"No!" Evolet heard himself scream in a voice that wasn't his own as he tripped over something or someone on the ground and flew the last feet, tackling Louis and bringing him to the ground before pitching into him as hard as he could.

Jason and Jasmine did the same thing with Ayan, who was stronger than either of them but not than both. On the other hand, Evolet and Louis were pretty well-matched, but Louis had already been fighting, and gradually Evolet found himself coming out on top.

A circumstance which changed when Louis panicked suddenly and fairly threw the twenty-year-old off and away from him.

Before Evolet could recover, the maniac was yelling something to the children who'd survived, and to Ayan, who now somehow broke free from Jasmine and Jason and bolted off into the darkness.

Everyone was gone. Everyone except for the casualties.

Evolet got up slowly, having rolled quite a distance over some rocky ground. He picked up his phone in hopes of calling the police, then realized: firstly, there were police scattered all over, either unconscious or dead; and secondly, his phone screen was shattered into bits, rendering the device completely useless.

Sighing, he dropped it carefully into his pocket, and looked around—and then it hit him for the first time that his parents and "Aunt Joyce" were on the ground, too—helpless and seemingly unconscious.

He'd never really heard Jasmine screaming before, but now he did, as she ran over to her mother. Evolet forced himself to follow her, shaking his head in a desperate effort to make the facts register. No, superhumans couldn't die.

But could they?

He couldn't go to see her. From a distance, Violet looked so pale and limp that Evolet was scared. So he went over to Conner first. He'd seen Conner alive—most definitely alive. But now as he bent down, ignoring the rocks and uneven surfaces, he wasn't so sure.

He took off his jacket instinctively, wiping off his father's face. Thank heavens, there were only a few gashes, nothing serious-looking. Evolet tried to staunch the bleeding lower down. Gradually it slowed, but Conner was still unconscious.

Evolet glanced up, feeling a cut on his own face closing up, and looked over to where Jason was on the phone.

His uncle sensed that he was looking at him, and lowered the phone, shaking his head. "No service. I'll have to run down. Hold the fort, will you two?"

Nodding, afraid to talk for fear his voice might betray the fact that he was near tears, Evolet turned back to his father, hoping and praying desperately that he would wake up.

He glanced around again, at the policemen who hadn't had a chance against superhuman opponents, at the few children who lay limp and motionless, obviously past rescuing. But he made himself get up and go over to inspect them.

He realized with a burst of shock that he recognized the four-year-old—Dawn Leblanc.

Evolet really did start crying then. How could the two maniacs have done this to the children?

Somehow he got up and went to find Jasmine and Violet. Jasmine was busy bandaging her mother's various wounds as best as she could with limited supplies, and she didn't look up as Evolet came by.

"I don't know," she answered his unspoken question tersely. "Where's Jason? We can get Mom down the mountain, but we should get an ambulance."

"He's gone for help," Evolet replied mechanically. He sat down. "Jaz, there are kids out there. Ayan and Louis were using *kids*."

Jasmine still didn't look up, but suddenly went motionless. "Did any escape?" she breathed.

"I don't think so." Evolet drew a long, deep, shuddering breath.

Jasmine put the last touches to a bandage, glancing closely at her mother's blank face before she stood up. "Well then. How's Dad look?"

"Not good," Evolet admitted. "But I patched him up."

"Joyce?" Jasmine went on as a matter of fact, heading over to where the American paratrooper lay prostrate, near the edge of the light.

"Aren't you worried about the policemen and the kids, too?" Evolet had to ask, following her dazedly.

"Can't you see that it's too late for them?" Jasmine hissed in a broken and distracted voice.

"But—"

"Shut up, shut up! I can't handle this, Evolet." Jasmine stopped suddenly, and her hands flew to her face. "Just let me think. Go take care of someone else. And shut up."

"I—"

"Are you two Whytes?" came a sudden voice behind them, and they wheeled around.

It was a tall, twelve-year-old boy. He'd just climbed out of a tree, a rifle slung over his back, his clothes torn and his face and hands smeared with dirt. His flaming red hair was long and rumpled, faintly tingled with blond, and there were purple scars on his face and arms. His eyes seemed part coral, part green.

He stared at the two almost dully, an atmosphere of fatigue and pain clinging to him.

They didn't answer.

They didn't need to. He'd already recognized them.

"I'm Michael Leblanc."

fifteen

"They're on life support and seem to be healing slowly. We understand you guys probably want to spend more time with them. But seriously, we need you," the Army Major said, glancing hard at the three standing in front of his desk. "We have to take care of Staunton and Monet ASAP. Jason Foley, we're putting you in charge, see?"

The Major fixed him with a penetrating stare. "I understand you'll be working with the Whyte kids?"

"Yeah, we'll be working together, or at least these two will," Jason clarified, wondering dimly if Alison and Charles would be coming on the expedition. "Is there anything else we need to know?"

"No—except, again, the safety of the children needs to be assured. We can't have anything like that happen again," the Major emphasized.

Jason nodded, as did Evolet and Jasmine. "Right. Will do."

Five minutes later the three were outside, heading for Jason's car, while Jasmine fumed.

"*Now* they ask us for help, after Mom and Dad and Aunt Joyce get totaled! Why didn't they ask us before? We could've gone with Mom and Dad, and—"

"—Gotten totaled as well," Jason cut in shortly. "Let's head back home to talk this over. —Is Michael still in the car?" he asked in amazement as he opened the driver's seat door and peered in.

The boy they'd found three nights before was sitting in the back seat, still looking exhausted. He glanced up as the Whytes and their uncle piled in, Evolet sitting next to him. He grinned at the boy, but the grin dissolved when it didn't meet with a similar reaction.

"Hey, Mike," Jason greeted the boy with an attempt at cheerfulness.

"Hi," Michael mumbled back. He closed his eyes as Jason started the car.

"Why didn't you come in?" Jasmine asked quietly. "It was cooler inside."

He just shrugged. Evolet gave him a worried look.

"You okay, man?" he asked.

Michael opened his eyes, but he didn't answer the question. Instead, he asked one of his own.

"Can I help you guys beat them?"

* * *

They'd gotten the entire story from him during the long and exhausting car ride from Nevada to Annapolis. He told them about the kidnapping, his eyes shut the entire time. And then about how Louis and Ayan had given him and Dawn and the others T6, the training in Nevada, and finally the trap.

"We didn't want to fight. But at the end of two weeks we were all insane," he explained on the flight back to Nevada to go after Louis and Ayan and the rest of the children. "I think I was the...only one left." He shuddered.

"And you say the T6 is still—doing that?" Jasmine asked quietly from the row in front. She was sitting there with Jason, and Evolet sat next to Michael. Michael had insisted on being allowed to help.

Michael nodded briefly. "Yeah, it is, and I don't think it's going to stop. It didn't stop for Ayan, did it?"

"Yeah, but..." Evolet broke off, shaking his head hopelessly. "I can't believe it. But you're stronger than me."

The twelve-year-old frowned. "Sometimes I feel like I can do anything just to make it stop. It scares me. I don't want to be like this."

"But you're not giving in," Jason reminded him. "You can handle this."

Michael shook his head. "I dunno how long. But if I can handle it, I'll be the first. Really, I—"

"Don't think about it that way," Jasmine interrupted him. "You can do this. And guess what? My dad got T6 and recovered."

"But he already had T4," Evolet pointed out before he could think. He caught his breath, realizing Jasmine was probably going to tell him off for his lack of tactfulness—later.

"So what?" Jasmine shrugged. "We can probably get Mike and the other kids a dose of T4 later—something like that. It'll be fine." She twisted around enough to smile at Michael, who returned it faintly.

"I don't know," he mumbled, his coral-green eyes downcast. "It gets stronger whenever I fight. I feel like there's a monster in me, that is trying to get out and take control. I don't want that to happen." He wasn't small for his age, but he seemed to shrink.

"Hey, it's gonna be fine," Evolet told him softly. "You're going to be okay, and we're all going to be alright."

Michael didn't look convinced, but he conceded the point. "Can I ask you guys something?" he asked after a few minutes.

"Fire away," Jasmine urged.

"How is it that you superhumans seem to keep getting into fights?" the boy asked slowly. "The Purple Blitzkrieg, and... I heard about something with Staunton some years later. At least, *he* talked about something. And wasn't there a climax five years ago?"

"Yeah, we see a lot of action in our lives," Evolet agreed. "The Purple Blitzkrieg involved my mom. Then five years ago was the incident with Louis and then Zaire Keswick. And now... Ayan, and Louis again."

"But you don't seem like normal humans," Michael muttered.

Jasmine's eyebrows shot up. "We aren't."

"No, I know, what I mean is that—" It took Michael a moment to get his words back into order. "You guys seem to live your own lives. You have fights, and small wars, and we pretty much ignore you. I mean, everyone else does." He gestured vaguely. "Normal people try not to get involved. It's like you're another race or something. A tiny country all on your own."

"Well, that's life for us, and I'm sorry you had to get dragged into it," Jason told him seriously. "But I think you're one of us now."

"Don't worry, it's not as exciting most of the time," Jasmine assured the twelve-year-old, grinning. "Unless you decide to go into the vigilante business. Like Alison."

"She's your sister, right?" Michael asked curiously.

"Yeah, twin," Jasmine admitted. "Though we don't act like it."

"And then your dad has a twin, too, right?" Michael continued.

"That's right," Evolet nodded.

"Cool!" Michael breathed. "I used to wish I had a twin."

Jasmine suddenly burst into laughter. "Evolet! Imagine if Mom had a twin?"

"Oh, no." Evolet paled. "Uncle Jason, does she?"

"I don't know," their uncle admitted laughingly. "But anyway, we're almost there. Everyone got everything?"

sixteen

"I have it ready, enough for the three. It works, I assure you. I call it—Schwann3."

The speaker was a tall, auburn-haired young woman of twenty-five, with blue-green eyes that glittered coldly whenever she wasn't smiling, but laughed when she was.

And she was smiling now. She was dressed in a casual leather jacket, black skirt, and high laced leather boots, her long hair done up in a bun with strategic flyaways.

Her name was Eternyti Schwann.

"Schwann3." The man behind the desk, a heavy-built, middle-aged U.S. Army Major, frowned. "Why Schwann3?"

"Schwann was the name of the machine used to maintain the Violet Army suits during the Purple Blitzkrieg." Eternyti's voice was crisp, and she took on the air of a kindergarten teacher as she condescendingly continued: "Schwann2 is, as you know, a compound used to terminate T4 and T5. And Schwann3 is the ultimate cure, Major Arcilla. Schwann helped; Schwann2 destroys; Schwann3 simply cures."

"You talk like T4, T5, hyper-T5, and T6 are all dangerous sicknesses." Major Lucius Arcilla folded his hands on his desk pensively. He looked up at the young woman standing in front of him, obviously waiting for an answer.

And she had one ready. "Yes, Major. In a way, they're all like viruses. They take over a human's body. That's why it's a crime to inject oneself. And that's why they're dangerous."

She frowned. "People with a strain of T4—they aren't human. They're another species. We have to understand that, to understand why they need a cure. It's for their own good, and for ours—for the good of the entire human race. What was the Violet Army's goal, Major Arcilla?"

He looked only slightly amused. "Well?"

"To wipe inferiors off the face of the planet," Eternyti told him. "It's only a matter of time until another 'superhuman' takes it into their head to do that very same thing. Luck may not be with us then. And we will not have a cure or a weapon."

"We have Schwann2," the Major broke in.

Eternyti shook her head emphatically. "No, Major—that's another way T4 is like a virus. As we've seen with T6, it can change so that our weapons will not affect it. If we leave it to spread, we'll only end up with more strains on our hands. It's bad enough already."

Finally Lucius shrugged. "Well then. What do you want me to do about it, Doctor Schwann?"

She smiled.

"Let me test my cure on the three who are in the hospital. Conner Whyte, Violet Whyte, and Joyce Liszt. And then we can work from there. If it doesn't work—well then, too bad. If it does—all well and good. But it's going to work, trust me."

* * *

"Michael, if you can't handle it, then you don't need to be here," Evolet told Michael Leblanc, three days later in Colorado.

They'd located Louis, Ayan, and the six remaining children finally, and were about to close in, backed up by a team of SWAT. Michael had managed to stay with Evolet, Jasmine, and Jason thus far, but now Evolet could see that he was getting strained. And he didn't want Michael to be overwhelmed. That could prove disastrous.

But the boy shook his head. "I'm fine," he insisted, looking Evolet in the eye. "Let's just finish this."

Sighing, Evolet looked away from the twelve-year-old and back at the building in front of them. It was a low, flat-roofed warehouse, the sort that Ayan and Louis liked to take over and use for their own purposes. The building was surrounded.

Everyone there knew that it was going to be the final battle. Evolet was with Michael on this side, and Jasmine and their uncle were on the other. It was during the last few minutes of the countdown; they would attack simultaneously.

It was an intimidating prospect to run into a building like that and meet whatever Louis and Ayan might have ready for them.

But Evolet was impatient for it to be over and done with already. He wanted to get it over with, go back home to Annapolis, and check on his parents. The last he'd heard, they were still unconscious.

But duty called, and here he was, waiting.

He glanced down at his chest. He, like the others, had four syringes strapped there, ready to be used.

They would knock out the children, and/or Ayan and Louis, for about five minutes, long enough to get them outside the building and contained. It was Evolet's, Michael's, Jasmine's, and Jason's job to do the knocking-out. The police were there simply to back them up.

Checking his watch, Evolet noticed that they had about fifteen seconds left. He motioned to Michael to be ready.

Three, two, one...

Two policemen aimed high-strength blasters at the door, blowing it off its hinges. Yelling to Michael to follow him, Evolet charged in ahead of the police, only to find himself in a large, empty storage room. But he spotted a door at the other end.

"This way," he shouted to his T6-ified companion, running over. He opened the door—and found the six children.

They were alone there; he couldn't see Ayan or Louis anywhere. Somewhat distractedly, he injected the first of them as they all cowered away, seemingly terrified. He hated to do it. But it was better for them that they be knocked out and wake up somewhere safe later.

A few seconds more, the job was done, and the police were evacuating the children. Michael and Evolet found themselves alone.

"That was too easy," Evolet muttered, shaking his head. "*Way* too easy."

"Where are Louis and Ayan?" Michael asked as they began to head back outside into the sunny summer day.

Evolet shrugged. "No clue."

They found the other two superhumans outside as well, just as confused.

"Empty," Jason reported. "Looks cleaned out."

"Well, we found the kids," Evolet returned. "But no one's left the building, right? So Ayan and Louis have to be in there."

"Right," Jasmine began, but just then one of the policemen started calling for help. The kids were waking up sooner than expected, and things weren't ready for them yet.

Evolet made a swift decision. "I'll go look for them—if I find them I'll call you. Go help with the kids, okay? I'll be right back." And he dashed off in the direction of the building again.

"Idiot," Jasmine mumbled, but she turned around to go deal with the situation anyway.

Eventually, they had everything taken care of, but Evolet still hadn't come out of the building.

Jasmine was about to go in after him when she realized one of the police was trying to catch her attention, a tall brunette standing some distance away from the building and working on a laptop. She glanced up again as Jasmine approached.

"Miss Whyte? The building is clear, right?"

"Umm, yeah, except for my brother," Jasmine nodded. "Why—"

"We've detected explosives inside." The policewoman cleared her throat nervously. "I was just thinking—"

"Hang it," Jasmine gasped. "One minute, I've got to get Evolet out of there then." Ignoring the policewoman, who nodded understandingly, Jasmine took an intercom out of her pocket. She pressed the PTT.

"Evy?"

She released it. Nothing.

"Evy? You need to answer."

Still nothing.

Groaning in desperation, Jasmine pulled her phone out of her pocket and dialed her older brother's number, walking quickly towards the building as she did so. She waited impatiently for an answer, and finally got one.

"Hi? Hey?—"

"Hey, it's me," she broke in quickly. "Evy—"

"—Hello? Oh sorry, can't hear you. I think it's me. Or...no? Yes? No? Maybe so? Heh but this is voicemail so go ahead and leave a message thank you—"

The dial tone. Jasmine narrowly avoided smashing her phone on the rocky pavement as she dashed forward in a panic to alert her brother in person.

"Evolet! WHY!"

seventeen

Evolet went through the entire building without finding Ayan or Louis, hearing static through his radio at one point and then turning it off. But he was just going through a second time when he stopped suddenly, in the middle of a high-roofed, raftered storage room in the center of the warehouse. Something was off. He felt it. More truthfully, he just sensed it.

After a moment's hesitation, he looked up, seeing the thick beams that held up the roof. And then something moved on one of them.

It was just the slightest movement, producing only the tiniest sound, but Evolet heard it, and looked back down so that the person above couldn't see his face. He smiled slightly. He wasn't alone.

Walking casually over to the door, he tensed, and then used the door frame to pull himself up, grabbing one of the rafters in a reckless leap. With a single, smooth motion, he swung himself up and crouched on the plank, breathing lightly.

He could see the other person now—except there were two of them. And both were aware of him.

Evolet snatched his phone out of his pocket and dialed Jasmine's number. Hoping she'd answer, he shoved the device back in and then moved precariously along the beam closer to the center of the room. The other two just watched him as if they thought he couldn't see them.

He managed a short laugh. "Come and get me! At least you can't jump down on me from there, Louis—your favorite thing to do, right?"

With a muttered expletive, one of the two figures leaped forward, crawling—no, running—along the thick beam. Evolet timed his reaction carefully, fully aware that the floor about twenty feet below them was made of concrete.

Once Louis got close enough, Evolet pushed him off the rafter, simply and easily. Louis went into free fall, grasping uselessly for a handhold that didn't exist. His wordless scream was cut short when he abruptly hit the concrete floor.

With a grim smile, Evolet advanced on Ayan, who up until this point hadn't moved. But now the African was looking clearly dubious, glancing first at his colleague on the floor and then at his enemy.

Evolet stopped, halfway across the rafter, realizing that he would only be playing into the maniac's hands if he got any closer. But Ayan seemed to judge that he was close enough, and, yelling something in African-accented French, he flipped across the short remaining distance between the two, knocking Evolet off the rafter in turn.

Evolet grabbed the rafter with one hand just in time to save himself, and dangled a moment, then got a hold on the wooden beam with his other hand.

He hung there a few seconds longer, then slowly but surely lifted himself up, finally getting back onto the beam.

Ayan was waiting, standing up, and now he kicked at Evolet before he'd fully gotten up, in the hope of making him lose balance while he was still in his precarious position.

Evolet was ready for him, though, and suddenly shook the beam violently, a plan that backfired as he himself fell off, barely managing to grab the beam again. He looked up to see Ayan's foot coming down on his hand.

Bracing himself for the sudden pain which came a moment later, Evolet gritted his teeth and jerked himself back up, shoving Ayan with all his might and then following up the move with a series of kicks and punches.

With an unearthly screech, Ayan followed his friend to the ground.

Evolet clung to the beam, panting as he looked down. He was going to have to drop. But as long as he wasn't being thrown off or anything he should make it.

He wondered suddenly why Jasmine hadn't answered the call. Sitting down on the beam, with his legs dangling, he pulled the device out of his pocket and turned the screen on.

That was just before a huge explosion rocked the entire building, and the roof and the supports blew away—and Evolet with them.

* * *

He woke up a few minutes later to a splitting headache, the worst he'd ever had, even compared to when Zaire had played ping-pong with him against a concrete wall.

There was a cut on the back of his head, and everything hurt incredibly. He felt like he'd definitely broken something.

But Jasmine was there now, bending over him with an anxious face. "Hey Evy, you awake now?"

"Guess so," he mumbled, trying to sit up but falling back helplessly. "I—uh—what happened?" he asked weakly, touching his head gingerly.

Having assured herself that her brother was alive, Jasmine contented herself with a wry smile. "The warehouse blew up. You're the only survivor... That's *if* you survive," she added, grinning.

"I might," he warned her, closing his eyes and trying to ignore the waves of aching pain that were gradually getting slower and less intense. "You'd better watch out. I just might."

"Don't worry, they're getting an ambulance," she told him.

It was the wrong thing to say, and Evolet's eyes flew open. He did sit up this time. "No ambulance. I'm not going to the hospital!" He shook his head, closing his eyes again until the dizzy feeling wore off.

"Whatever," Jasmine mumbled. Then, as if remembering something, she pointed to his phone some distance away. "Why didn't you get my call?"

"Why didn't you get mine—" Evolet broke off suddenly as he realized his phone was smashed into approximately two billion pieces. "Oh—"

"How many phones has he broken now?" Jason wondered, coming up behind the two.

Evolet grinned weakly at him. "This makes six, I think. Wait, Jaz—did you say I was the only survivor? What about—"

She shook her head. "No, Louis and Ayan didn't make it out."

"And that means—" Evolet broke off for a moment, remembering. "That means we're done here. Finally! When do we go back home?"

eighteen

"M—Mom?"

Evolet couldn't believe what he was seeing. *Whom* he was seeing.

It was his mother, of course. Violet Whyte, née Arnnu or Foley.

But she was nothing like she'd been in all the years he'd known her. Only six, to be precise—but still. He'd never thought she could be like this.

Jasmine was in a similar state of shock. But Violet smiled at them. "So you two won?"

She looked decades older than she was. Her face was gray and wrinkled, and when she talked there was something curiously wavery in her voice.

Evolet couldn't believe it. She was in a *wheelchair*.

"*Mom*," he choked again, and this time he could go on. "What happened to you?"

Violet shook her head slowly, and her smile disappeared. "They found a cure, Evy. Or that's what they call it."

"A cure?" Jasmine echoed, shaking her head in disbelief. "They call this a cure?"

"They say I'll be out of the wheelchair eventually," Violet told them slowly. "But you guys won? Where's Jason?"

"He's with Michael," Evolet replied, still somewhat distracted.

"Michael?" Violet tilted her head interrogatively.

"Michael Leblanc. Oh, you haven't heard, have you? One of the kids who got kidnapped. He joined us," Evolet explained quickly. "And yes, we won."

"Well?" Violet clicked her tongue expectantly. "Tell me about it!"

And so Evolet sat down on the hospital bed, giving his mother a long and detailed narration of the fight. She listened intently.

After a few minutes, Jasmine discovered she was being ignored. Which definitely suited her purpose at this point.

She walked around the hospital room quietly, looking for traces of the so-called "cure." It was relatively clean, just like any other normal hospital room. But after confirming that the others weren't paying attention to her, Jasmine discreetly lifted the lid of the trash can.

There was what she was looking for. A box labeled *Schwann3*. And even better—the papers from it.

After another glance back at her brother and mother, she pulled them out and sat down on the window seat to read them over.

* * *

Half an hour later, Jasmine and Evolet were leaving the hospital, Jasmine armed with the papers safely in her pocket.

Evolet was so absorbed in thinking about his parents—they'd gone to visit Conner as well—that he didn't notice Jasmine's hard, angry, and determined expression as she got into the back seat without a word.

Evolet drove them to Moira's house, and the entire ride was passed in silence. Well, most of it. Then Jasmine spoke up, about five minutes away.

"Evy, it's not a cure."

He was somewhat surprised to hear her voice, but he didn't show it. "It isn't?"

"Isn't that obvious?" she asked him, something sarcastic in her voice. "Mom's in a wheelchair. Dad can barely walk. They both look so old. Older than they should be. And Dad forgot your name!"

"Depends on how you look at it," Evolet had to admit. "But if they were trying to get rid of T4 I think they succeeded pretty well."

"Evy, that's not the point," Jasmine told him urgently. "It's not a cure, and T4 doesn't need cured anyway. Mom and Dad should've been pretty well on the way to recovery by now. You were blown clear of an exploding building, and you're fine now. But Schwann3 is weakening them, Evy!"

Evolet nodded seriously. "But it's too late now. And Mom and Dad seem fine with it."

"That's because they're tired—and hurting—and they can't seem otherwise," Jasmine returned. "But that's not all, Evy. They mean to give *us* Schwann3, too."

Her older brother's face tensed. Keeping his eyes on the road, he parked by the curb opposite Moira's house. "How do you know that?"

"Talk later," she replied, popping her door open and fairly dashing across the street and up the steps to Moira's house, flipping over a passing car's roof on her way. Shaking his head, Evolet followed her, though in a less spectacular manner.

He found her in the front hallway, talking avidly with Moira. "Alison and Charles? They're both gone? Where?"

"Eternity Labs, Texas," Moira returned, nodding briefly to Evolet as he came in behind Jasmine. "They got a government summons. Welcome home."

"Eternity Labs? You're kidding." Jasmine did a facepalm. "When?"

* * *

"So, since they're not answering the phone, and they've had enough time to get there by now," Jasmine was telling Evolet about five minutes later, back in the car, "we can assume they have arrived and—been detained. We're probably going to get a summons any minute now. Us—and Uncle Jason, and Michael, and...everyone else with T4."

She was right, as they found out when they got to the doctor's office, where Jason had taken Michael to see if there was anything that might help with the T6. The two were just heading out as Evolet and Jasmine were heading in, and they bumped into each other—literally.

"Done visiting?" Jason asked Evolet quickly. "Yes? Good. I was about to call you to pick us up."

"Find anything for Mike?" Evolet wondered absentmindedly.

"Not really." Jason shook his head and sighed. "We should get someone working on it. Speaking of which, I just got a summons to—"

"Eternity Labs, Texas," Jasmine interjected. "We're still waiting for ours."

Following Evolet and Michael out to the car, Jason gave his niece a startled look. "What's going on?"

* * *

"It's run by Eternyti Schwann," Jasmine explained on the way to the airport, two hours later. "She—"

"She's the one your mother sent Conner's blood to for testing," Jason interrupted. "But go on."

The man was paying more attention to the road than he usually did, his face hard-set and grim. Evolet was sitting in the passenger seat, staring at a picture on his phone. A picture of the entire Whyte family, with the addition of Jason, taken a few months before.

Evolet was lost in reverie, staring at his parents. He couldn't believe that Conner walked with a cane and Violet was in a wheelchair. It was just completely, totally, impossible.

"Why are we getting called there?" Michael wanted to know.

Jasmine glanced at him and smiled briefly. It wasn't often that Michael Leblanc spoke up.

"You don't really want to know," she muttered, sobering up again and feeling in her pocket for the papers she'd taken from the hospital.

"Guess we'll find out," Jason returned, unconsciously much like his sister-in-law Moira.

Evolet looked up, startled before it registered that the voice was Jason's. "Oh come on," he mumbled, turning off his phone's screen—his *new* phone's screen—and sliding it into his pocket.

Sighing resignedly and settling back in his seat, Evolet reflected that he'd been doing more traveling lately than ever before. And they had thirty minutes left to go before they arrived at the airport—just in time to catch the flight that had been scheduled for them—in a private airplane. It would be his first time—though not Jasmine's, and not Jason's either, if the Victor aircraft counted as a private flight.

"I guess I can just tell you guys later," Jasmine shrugged.

She, too, leaned back. The last few days had been hectic.

Michael's eyebrows shot up as he turned to look at her briefly but made no comment. He might not be related to them, but at this point he knew the Whytes and Foleys enough to tell when they were hiding something important.

At this point, it looked like Michael might become a part of the family. He went everywhere with Jason, who was considering adopting the boy if such a thing became necessary.

No one had taken any real notice of Michael, except this new summons to Texas.

On the other hand, the remaining other six kids had been taken charge of by the police right away and shipped off—to Texas, presumably.

"How long will it take to get to Texas?" the twelve-year-old wondered aloud, after a few seconds of bored, awkward silence.

"Oh, a few hours." Jasmine gestured vaguely. "Say, Michael, when's your birthday?"

He could tell she was only asking the question to distract him, and perhaps herself as well, but he answered it anyway. His voice was quiet. "It's in about a week. June 3."

"Cool," she grinned. "Whatcha wanna do?"

nineteen

"Welcome to Eternity Labs, Mr. Foley, Mr. Whyte, Miss Whyte, Mr. Leblanc. Would you please step in here? Doctor Schwann will be right with you," the white-clad woman who looked like a nurse told them.

Jason nodded and followed her down the clean, crisp white hall to a waiting room. Evolet, Jasmine, and Michael stepped after him, all four of them completely alert and taking note of their surroundings.

From the outside, it had been obvious that Eternity Labs was a heavily secured laboratory facility. It was comprised of expansive grounds that were protected by ten-foot-high iron fencing. They'd been let in at the gate after an intense patting-down and identity verification, and had had to switch vehicles to a regulation van, which took them to the Eternity Labs Visitors & Patients Facility, where they were escorted into the building.

Here it seemed nice and homey, though with a public building aura—smooth tile floor, thick and strong-looking wood-paneled walls, and fire-extinguisher-implanted ceiling.

Jasmine's tall leather boots tapped quietly on the tiles as she walked along, just behind Evolet. There was AC on in the building—which was perfectly natural, as it was summer in Texas—but perhaps it was set to a degree or so too low for Jasmine's comfort, heightening her sense of danger in the air. She didn't shiver, but still she was perfectly aware of it. As were the others.

Each of the doors they passed was neatly labeled, and for every one of them there was no handle, but instead a place to slide an ID card, and Jasmine noticed motion sensors above each doorframe. The hallway was relatively deserted, though it went on for a good long way, possibly the entire length of the building.

Finally their guide stopped and pressed her hand on the door, roughly at face level. There was a soft click, and the door swung open of its own accord, stopping short of the wall on the other side. The woman stepped out of the doorway, smiling.

"Step right in, and Doctor Schwann will be in to see you in a few minutes," she assured them.

After a moment of hesitation, Jason walked into the room, followed by Evolet and Michael. Jasmine followed their example after another keen yet fleeting glance at the woman's so obviously fake smile.

Blinking as she crossed the threshold into the room, Jasmine set her own mouth in a firm, hard smile. Her hand crept instinctively up to her French coat pocket and she felt the papers there. Underneath the coat, she wore one of her mother's trademark purple jackets. She was ready.

Sitting down next to her older brother on a plain, gray sofa, she assessed her new surroundings instinctively.

"Nice place," Evolet remarked appreciatively. Jasmine nodded in agreement.

The room was spacious, lined with comfortable yet practical furniture, with a thick, red carpet that Jasmine's boots sunk into as she walked.

Now, as she sat down, she crossed her legs and leaned back against the couch cushions, sighing without realizing it.

Her light blue eyes flitted up to the walls, and after a startled intake of some modern art, she rolled them towards the ceiling in despair. There were two windows—barred over. The only other way of exit was through the door, as far as she could see. Finally, Jasmine closed her eyes, tapping her right hand against her knee impatiently.

"Remember, don't give away that we know anything," she murmured to the others, who all nodded in agreement, though she wasn't really paying attention to them.

The walls were thick, they realized a moment later when the door began to open and they suddenly heard the closing of a discussion that had just been going on in the hallway.

The toe of a smooth, black boot came around the corner of the door, and Jason, Evolet, Jasmine, and Michael stood up expectantly while listening in interest to the rest of the newcomer's sentence.

"—only be ten minutes or so, tell them that. And make sure everything's ready. Thanks, see you."

The four superhumans could have heard—no, registered—the quiet remark that followed, had they been listening for it, but they weren't.

Eternyti Schwann stepped into the room, slick and professional as always. Her mouth curved into a smile as she reached up with her right hand and brushed a curly auburn wisp off her shoulder.

The door shut silently behind her, and Eternyti glanced over her visitors quickly, from Jason Foley to Michael to Jasmine and Evolet.

Michael had his eyes closed. Jason and Jasmine watched Eternyti. But Evolet met Eternyti's gaze, startling her. He looked older than he was, and she had to remind herself that he was only twenty. For a moment she'd thought he was her age.

"Welcome! It's good to see you here. I've been looking forward to meeting the heroes of the last week!" she greeted them, stepping energetically across the room to shake Jason's hand, and then Michael's, and Jasmine's and Evolet's.

Jason and Michael held back, she could tell. But when Jasmine's turn came the Whyte girl pumped the scientist's hand emphatically, making Eternyti glad to have her hand back. In fact, she was slightly intimidated, but after another glance at the friendly smile on Jasmine's face, the scientist dismissed the brief sensation of hostility. She went on to shake Evolet's hand somewhat distractedly and motioned for them all to sit.

"Good to meet you, too, Doctor," Jason returned politely.

Eternyti's smile broadened, and she took a seat next to Michael on a wide blue sofa. He ignored her, staring into space.

"This is a really cool laboratory," Evolet spoke up after a scarcely distinguishable moment of silence. "What do you do here, Dr. Schwann?"

She glanced up, still smiling, but not failing to notice that he was looking rather intently at her—with the slightest hint of a smirk on his face. She returned the look.

"Oh, not too much, Mr. Whyte. We have a hospital for patients with incurable illnesses—I mean, incurable until we find the cure. For every evil there is a cure," she added suddenly, glancing across the room at Jasmine. "Which is why I asked you all to come visit me here. It was really quite kind of you to do so. I'm sure you know why—"

"Yes, you've found a cure for T4, and—the other three," Evolet nodded, looking somewhat more interested. He took his hand out of his hair, and dropped it on his lap distractedly. Michael looked like he was going to fall asleep.

"But we do have a lot to talk about," Eternyti went on, ignoring the interruption. "Would you guys like some tea? Or coffee, perhaps?"

"We could just—" Evolet began, an impatient tone creeping into his voice—but Jasmine stepped on his foot suddenly, hard.

He pulled a face at her, cringing momentarily. If anything could hurt his feet, albeit slightly, it was another superhuman stepping on them, in hard, tough boots.

"No thanks," Jasmine told Eternyti, smiling innocently as if she hadn't just forcibly silenced her older brother. "I don't really like tea or coffee."

"I'll take a coffee," Jason shrugged, closing his eyes briefly.

Eternyti nodded, standing up. "I assume that means neither Evolet nor Michael would like anything?" she asked lightly, glancing down at the boy.

Michael had pulled his legs up onto the seat and was staring hard at the floor, but he shook his head. "No thanks," he mumbled in a very obviously preoccupied voice.

As Eternyti began walking towards the door, her hand happened to brush against Michael's, and she tensed for a moment. It felt like he was running a very high fever. But then she remembered Violet's enumeration of the Conner's previous T6 symptoms, and she dismissed the startling detail.

Crossing the room to the door, Eternyti put her hand in the center, and stepped out when it opened. It shut behind her.

"Creep" was the first thing anyone said—Jasmine.

Evolet glanced at her, surprised. "Creep?"

"Shh, they can probably hear us in here," Jason warned the two, and they nodded.

Evolet found himself running his hands through his hair again. "Wish she would just get to the point," he muttered. "I hate the suspense."

"Are you okay?" Jason asked Michael, his brow furrowing. "You seem more out of it than usual."

"I'm okay," Michael replied. "Just—hurting." He clenched his hands, and shut his eyes.

They fell silent, perhaps because there wasn't much more to be said, but perhaps also because the door started opening just then, and Eternyti came in. Jason stood up, and took his cup of coffee, while Eternyti sat down, on a seat of her own this time and with her own cup of tea.

"Well," she began finally, breaking the tense silence. "I guess we can begin."

twenty

"Yes, Mr. Evolet Whyte, you're right. We have found a cure for T4, T5, hyper-T5, and T6." Eternyti smiled. "Have you visited your parents recently? They're still in the hospital, I hear, after battling with that—uhh—tiger maniac?"

"Yeah, him and Louis Staunton." Evolet's eyes narrowed, despite the fact that Jasmine had warned him against letting Eternyti know they were aware of her plans. "But they're getting better. I mean, if you can call it better—ow!" Jasmine had stepped on his foot again. This time he glared at her.

"How did you develop it?" Jason asked, tactfully smoothing over the break as Eternyti turned to look at him.

She shrugged. "It didn't take long, with the resources we have here," she explained. "Anyway, I was very glad to hear that it worked. Michael, I hear you have T6?"

"You're saying it like it's a sickness, but yeah," Michael mumbled, not looking up.

"It is a sickness," Eternyti contradicted him, standing up. "Both physical and mental. I'm a doctor as well as a scientist, and I've studied it."

"With Dad?" Evolet asked softly.

The scientist shook her head, still looking at Michael. "No, with those children you four rescued from Monet and Staunton. But what am I saying? Michael Leblanc here is a child as well. Michael, do you know what T6 can do to you?"

She spoke to him in a kindergarten-teacher voice, and he looked up, annoyed. "Yes," he answered shortly, without going into details.

But Eternyti went into them anyway. "It gives you a perpetual, burning fever—which you know first-hand—and can also make you go insane—"

"He knows that," Evolet interrupted, raising his eyebrows.

Eternyti smiled slightly. "I know."

"What's happened to the other kids, by the way?" Jason wondered aloud. "Are they here?"

"Yes, they are here," Eternyti nodded. She didn't sit down again, but she did walk over to the wall by the door and lean against it. "They're in another building, in fact. Somewhat contained, seeing as they seem to have more side effects of T6 than Mr. Leblanc here—but we treat them well, of course. And then once we have enough of the cure ready for them, they'll be able to go home."

"Oh, it's not ready?" Evolet asked in surprise.

"Unfortunately, no." The scientist shook her head. "We came up with the formula for Schwann3 within twenty-four hours of receiving your father's blood sample. It took us about two weeks to actually produce it in enough quantities for testing, and what we gave to Conner Whyte, Violet Whyte, and Joyce Liszt was the very last of it. We started making more yesterday, but again, it won't be ready for two weeks. But we'll have enough for everyone."

"Everyone," Michael echoed dully. It was more of a statement than a question.

His older sister smiled. "Yes, everyone. That includes you, and all other superhumans, along with some surplus. I hope to convince the U.S. government to completely destroy all samples of T4 and its various strains. Then the trouble will be over."

The atmosphere in the room changed perceptively, though no one's expressions changed. Only Evolet looked up.

"And what if someone didn't want the cure?" he asked, and this time Jasmine didn't implement any silencing techniques.

Eternyti nodded, as if she'd been expecting the question. But she didn't answer it directly. "You see, Mr. Whyte—"

"Call me Evolet," he broke in. Evolet was not used to being called "Mr. Whyte"—that was his father's usual title.

She nodded again, distractedly. "You see, Evolet, T4, T5, hyper-T5, and T6 are all like viruses. They're a danger to the human race. You know the common cold?"

"Yeah," Evolet nodded. "Of course I do. I mean, I know *about* it," he corrected himself hastily as Jasmine shot him a suspicious glance, "even if I've never had it myself."

"Okay, well then, you're probably aware of the fact that it isn't just a single virus. It's a virus that changes every year, every attack. It mutates. Not into another species, but into another form of itself. And then when a human becomes infected with it, it tries to turn the human into itself. When it succeeds, it kills the human."

Eternyti sighed. "T4 and its strains are basically another virus, but the first one that actually succeeds in taking over the body without killing it. You could say people with T4 are no longer human, but a virus. A virus that spreads."

"Interesting," Evolet muttered. If he hadn't already been sure that Eternyti was wrong, he would have felt very uncomfortable. Him? A virus?

"And that is why we at Eternity Labs have produced a cure," the scientist went on as a matter of course. "We have to stop this T4—this virus—before it spreads or mutates any more. In other words, now."

"But that doesn't answer my question," Evolet broke in. "What if the— er—T4-ified human doesn't want to be cured? I mean, if T4 *is* a virus, it's a pretty useful and convenient one. Don't they have the right—"

"Viruses do not have rights," Eternyti cut in sharply, straightening so that she wasn't leaning on the wall anymore, but stood alert, one hand in the pocket of her leather jacket. "Viruses are one of the many threats to mankind's existence. It's a matter of luck that T4, T5, etc., only spread by means of blood contact. But how long will that last? This is why it must be stopped now, without delay."

"But—" Evolet began, then stopped as he was met with an oddly wry smile from the scientist.

"But of course, it's only natural that the virus would put up a fight," Eternyti went on slowly. "And a virus like T4 seems to have deliberately equipped itself with the necessary means to defend itself adequately and well.

But it still has to go."

And then Jasmine stood up and spoke for the first time, after a curious glance at her uncle, who seemed to be falling asleep, despite the fact that the conversation was quickly reaching a climax. "But there's something you don't understand," she told Eternyti urgently, and the blue-green eyes flew to her in surprise. "We aren't viruses. We are people. Like you and like everyone else. You can't do this to us."

"See—" Eternyti began, but Jasmine had had enough. She wasn't about to stop now.

"We have minds, and souls, and emotions, and feelings. We have rights as well. We're human. You have no right to contain us—"

Jasmine's eyes were flashing angrily, but much to her disgust Eternyti kept a composed and condescending voice as she broke in calmly with: "Menaces must be kept contained. Especially insane ones."

"I get your point about the other kids," Jasmine returned heatedly, "but we four here are not insane. Neither were Mom, nor Dad. Nor Joyce Liszt. They got injured working with the government to contain a real threat, and what did you do? You took advantage of that to inject them with your so-called cure! And now Mom's in a wheelchair, and Dad has memory loss, and you come in here with your talk of being dangerous and you want to do the same thing to us!"

"And what," Eternyti asked her softly, "of the six children who *are* insane? What would you have me do with them, then, eh? Let them stay that way? Michael can tell you how it feels—if he hasn't already."

Evolet drew breath in swiftly, standing up as well. He took up his stand next to Jasmine, both facing the scientist.

"He's told us. But one thing we know is that my dad recovered from T6. It was only a matter of time—for him, anyway." He clenched his fists, exhaling softly and noting with increased annoyance that Eternyti didn't seem intimidated in the least. But subconsciously he admired her for that.

"And guess what? There are worse things than temporary pain and insanity." Jasmine took up the argument. "Like a cure which can kill— Schwann3. You're not testing that thing on us, even if Mom and Dad did survive. You probably saw for yourself how it left them—weak and broken. What about the tests you ran on mice that failed? And then you tried it on my parents regardless! And look where they are now. You're not giving those kids Schwann3. You're not giving it to us, either. There has to be another way for them to recover. You're not going to sacrifice us to your theories!" Her eyes flashed fire.

Eternyti's smile widened, though only slightly, and she shook her head. "I'm sorry, Jasmine Whyte. It's true that my seeing T4 as a virus is only a theory. But what I'm seeing right now only confirms it. I'm going to hold to that theory until you disprove it."

She paused, looking up at the taller yet younger girl fearlessly. "You can't disprove a theory like that by attacking me, by the way. Even if I die, it will still be there. To me, you and the others are viruses—unless you find a scientific way to prove that you aren't."

"We understand that," Evolet hissed through clenched teeth.

"You do? Good, then." Eternyti's hand had been somewhat restless in her pocket, but now it stopped moving, holding something. "Then you also understand that according to my responsibility as a medical doctor I'm under obligation to protect the human population from threats. And—pardon me—but you, yes you, are a threat. So you understand why I do this."

She pulled her hand out of her pocket finally, to reveal a small device. With a quick, decisive motion, she pressed her right index finger firmly down on the small blue button, and then the superhumans in the room became aware of an alarm sounding faintly from the hallway.

twenty-one

Behind Evolet and Jasmine, Michael leaped to his feet, fully awake now that the climax had been reached. But Evolet stole a quick glance behind him, realizing suddenly with a burst of shock that Jason was slumped over, the cup of coffee placed neatly on the table beside him. Evolet gasped.

"You—" he began, turning again to look at Eternyti and then cutting short what he'd been going to say. The door was opening.

Nodding almost sympathetically to him, Eternyti stepped out the door, addressing a crowd of security who'd apparently been waiting outside. "Take all four, knock them out, and secure them in Building B3."

Evolet gave an incredulous little exclamation, froze momentarily, and threw himself at the blue-uniformed guards who now began to fill the doorway. Jasmine was already in motion; she yelled for Michael to get out the window as she joined her older brother in blocking the entrance.

Meanwhile Michael followed orders, darting to the other end of the room to the window. The windowsill was at about eye level for him, but he jumped up easily, grabbed hold of the bars, and peered out. It took him two seconds to punch out the glass. He would fit through the space, and he had no doubt but that he could handle the security guards that were now encircling the building. But he glanced back at Evolet and Jasmine, and then at the drugged Jason, and an expression of reckless resolve came over his face.

Grasping two adjoining metal bars tightly, he gave them a hard jerk. There was no apparent result besides the fact that Michael's face reddened from the exertion, but he continued to hold on to the bars, while he walked up the wall with his feet. Now he leaned back, holding himself up by means of the window bars but pushing against the wall with his feet.

The twelve-year-old took a deep breath, and then exerted full pressure on the wall while holding to the bars with his hands. He grunted loudly, gasping as the struggle between him and the bars wore on.

Suddenly they came loose in his hands, leaving jagged holes in the wall. Michael fell backwards onto the floor, flying about ten feet before he landed hard on his back, metal bars securely in his hands. He laughed, an out-of-breath, triumphant laugh, lying there for a moment before springing to his feet and dashing over to Evolet and Jasmine, who were occupied in sliding the door shut.

"Look," he yelled to them, and Evolet glanced at him briefly.

"Good," he grunted in approval, but it was enough, and Michael fairly beamed. "Get that sofa over here, will you?"

Nodding absently, Michael slid across the room to the sofa the Whyte siblings had been sitting on, dragging it over to the half-closed doorway. He and Evolet shoved it in front of the door, while Jasmine jumped back; then she leaped on top, kicking a dart gun away from someone who'd just been about to shoot through.

"Schwann2, I think!" she called to her companions, biting her lip and ducking another dart that flew into the room and lodged in the ceiling.

"LVK knockout," came Eternyti's unexpected contribution from down the hallway. Jasmine's eyebrows shot up, and she jumped up, grabbing the dart and throwing it futilely through the doorway gap towards where the voice had come from. She ducked then, and suddenly Evolet tapped her shoulder.

He spoke one word. "Move."

She leaped backward off the sofa, letting him up to stick the back of a chair through the gap. The breach was sufficiently blocked—for the time being. Jasmine, Evolet, and Michael glanced at each other, none of them even panting, though Michael's face was redder than usual.

"Window," Evolet commanded. "Michael first."

"They're shooting out there," he pointed out, running over to the window and preparing to jump up, gripping the edge of the windowsill tightly. He paused and looked back at Evolet expectantly.

Jasmine answered first. "Get onto the roof and get out of range. We'll meet you there and then break free."

Michael nodded, pulling himself up with a single, fluid movement, and then scrambling out of the window. Jasmine and Evolet stared at Jason, and then looked at each other dismally. He was still completely unconscious.

"Leave him," Evolet decided after a moment's intense thinking. He clenched his fists in annoyance. "He'll just get shot up out there, and we don't know when he'll wake up. But here he's safe for two weeks. We can rescue him and everyone else before then."

Jasmine nodded emphatically, her eyes lighting up. "Hang on, Evy, I have an idea! Hold the door," she instructed breathlessly, grabbing a scrap of paper out of her pocket and starting to write.

Evolet did a facepalm, but jumped over to the door anyway, just in time to shove the chair back in place from the security guards' attempts to dislodge it. He winced momentarily as a bullet came through one of the thinner areas of the cushioning and grazed his hand. "Hurry up, Jaz!"

"Almost there," she breathed, her pen moving like lightning across the paper in her nimble fingers. She stood up suddenly, then bent down again, swiftly tucking the paper into her uncle's shoes. "Got it!"

"About time," Evolet muttered, ducking another bullet and racing across the room to the window. Jasmine was already there, pulling herself up. A moment later she was out, then she jumped back up from the other side and from there grabbed the edge of the roof and jerked herself up. Evolet followed suit.

On the roof, they were easy targets for the security soldiers on the ground. Evolet, Jasmine, and Michael were all very glad of their bulletproof jackets, à la mode Violet Whyte. Evolet clenched his bleeding fist as he leaped from slate to slate, in advance of his two younger companions.

Bullets whizzed around them, and Michael ducked a couple with his super-human instinct that definitely came in handy at such moments. Nevertheless, he began to fall back, and as they neared the end of the first building's roof Jasmine glanced behind momentarily to check on him. She discovered he was panting, his face nearly as red as his hair.

"Mike!" she called above the gunshots that were still ringing out. "You okay?"

"I—"

She looked at him, realizing with a start that the coral color in his eyes had completely overtaken the green. "Mike!"

Evolet was already heading back. "Find us a route, Jaz—I'll carry him!"

Jasmine shrugged as her older brother shouldered the boy, and turned, speeding up drastically and then leaping the short gap between the Eternity Labs Visitors & Patients Facility and whatever was next to it. Looking ahead, she followed the slope of the roof, finding a spot to jump down where it wasn't too high and there weren't any guards nearby.

Meanwhile Evolet grabbed hold of the twelve-year-old superhuman, drawing in his breath sharply when he touched the bare skin of Michael's forearms. The boy was overwhelmingly warm. Perhaps over 120°.

Evolet winced, realizing first of all that he had accidentally smeared blood on Michael's clothes with his hand, and secondly that Michael's T6 was being unusually active at the moment. Like it did whenever the boy was fighting or under stress.

"Hang in there," he whispered to him. "Grab my shoulders. There you go. Hang on tight."

"Okay," came the boy's somewhat hoarse reply. Evolet bit his lip and charged on.

Barely making the jump, he slid down the edge of the next roof as Jasmine had, landing hard, what with Michael's extra weight. With the boy still on his back, he raced after Jasmine across the narrow strip of grass between the building and the tall iron fence.

Jasmine was already there, panting. She touched it lightly with the back of her hand and jumped away instinctively.

"Electric," she hissed to Evolet. "Gloves?"

He responded by pulling a couple of pairs of thick leather gloves out of his jacket pocket, which were there for such emergencies as this. Tossing two of the gloves to Jasmine, he pulled on the second pair himself, noting subconsciously that he was going to have to wash them out afterwards. After breathing a warning to Michael to keep hanging on, Evolet began to climb, Jasmine following in case he fell.

"Hurry up!" she shouted to him impatiently as she began to hear the first signs of pursuit from around the buildings.

Evolet merely grunted in reply, somehow making his hands go faster. His clothes were good protection against the electricity, but he was afraid that if he accidentally touched the metal with his bare skin he'd fall down from the electric shock, even if it wouldn't knock him out or kill him or anything like that.

He reached the top, again glad for his gloves as he discovered it was lined with barbed wire. Slowly he swung over, then suddenly became aware that Michael was slipping.

"Mi—!" Evolet yelled desperately, whipping one hand off the fence to steady his younger friend. Then his other arm had to take the weight of them both—and touched the fence.

"*OWW!*" Evolet shrieked, more from shock than from pain—a shriek which continued as he fell backwards on top of Michael, down the thirty feet all the way to the ground, which was, thankfully, covered in grass.

He rolled off the smaller boy instantly and sat up, looking him over. Michael's eyes were closed, but they fluttered open and stared vaguely at Evolet as he proceeded to shake Michael violently. "Wake up!"

"'M awake," Michael mumbled.

Evolet noted anxiously that the boy's eyes were still completely coral-colored. "Mike—"

"Move," Jasmine broke in, shoving Evolet aside to get to the boy. She pushed Michael's sleeve up, and pulled a small syringe out of her pocket, knocking off the cap and then gently sliding the needle into Michael's forearm. Slowly she injected the tube of almost clear, pale white fluid.

"And that is—?" Evolet raised his eyebrows as she dropped the syringe on the ground and pulled Michael up roughly.

"It's the opposite of adrenaline, Evy. Hope Eternyti isn't anti-litter," Jasmine muttered to herself. "Well, she can clean it up herself. We're in a hurry. Come on, Mike—we have to go."

Evolet turned to see crowds of Eternity Lab guards racing for the fence.

"Yeah, let's get out of here!"

twenty-two

"Not to worry, I knew this was going to happen," Eternyti remarked calmly, glancing into the messy room once her guards had cleared the doorway. She tilted her head thoughtfully, looking at the still unconscious Jason. "They'll be back."

"Where do we put him?" someone asked.

Eternyti waved her hand vaguely. "The Containment Facility, in a Class 3 room. Not too far from Alison, Charles, Christina, Flynn, and Petyr. But make sure security is at its highest, from now on. Don't bother to chase after the three that got away; just call the police and let things sit. They'll be back, I know."

"Wait, stop," she ordered suddenly, and the two guards who'd begun to carry Jason out of the room paused and looked at her in surprise.

"Yes?"

"What's that?" the scientist demanded, pointing to the corner of a piece of paper that was sticking out from one of the superhuman's shoes.

Someone grabbed it, and handed it to her. Eternyti unfolded the paper, reading it twice. Her eyebrows shot up, and she crumpled the paper, dropping it into her pocket.

"Keep going," she told the porters quietly. "But before you lock the place down, one of you come to my office. I'm going to give you another note to replace this one."

* * *

"They got away cleanly," a security guard reported to Eternyti about half an hour later. "The fence wasn't a high enough voltage, apparently. Should we increase it?"

Eternyti shook her head. "No, not for now. Can you get Major Lucius Arcilla on the phone in my office for me, please? I'll be right there."

The guard nodded, saluted, and rushed away. Eternyti followed at her own pace, but was accosted by another guard a few minutes later.

"Doctor Schwann—we're ready for the note now."

"One moment," Eternyti breezed, pulling the paper out of her pocket and uncrumpling it. She rushed to another, empty office room, and laid the note on the desk, pulling out a new sheet of paper and a pencil. Pausing reflectively for about three seconds, she began to write.

Finally, a minute or so later, she'd finished. She handed the original paper to the guard, keeping her own copy for herself.

"Stick that where he'll find it, but make sure you don't 'notice' it for an hour or so after he wakes up," she instructed him, her blue-green eyes calm and confident. "And make sure the building is completely locked down. Got that?"

"Got it." This guard, too, saluted, and hurried off.

Eternyti continued on her way to her normal office, finally reaching it and taking the phone from another security officer who notified her quietly that Major Arcilla was on the line. She nodded to him, and he left the room, shutting the door behind him.

"Good afternoon, Major. Yes, this is Doctor Schwann. I'm well, and you?"

Eternyti smiled lightly as she listened to the Major's reply.

"Yes. Actually, I wanted to speak to you about that. The two Whytes, Jason Foley, and Michael Leblanc did show up—but Michael and the Whytes got away. Do you think you can look for them discreetly? ... But not right away. We won't have more Schwann3 for two weeks. I'll try to hurry it up, but I'm not sure if I can.

"No, I don't think I need reinforcements here. But can you do a favor for me? ... Can you censor Conner and Violet Whyte, and let me know if anything comes up? I think I know what their next move is going to be... Yes, this is my number. Thanks. Goodbye!"

* * *

At the same time, Michael was fast asleep in a cave some distance away from Eternity Labs, lying on his jacket against the rocky cavern wall. A few feet away, Evolet and Jasmine discussed their plans in hushed tones.

"I told him not to worry but to be ready to break out, and to get news to Ali and Charles and—his siblings and Christina Fletcher, if he gets the chance," Jasmine was explaining. "I only hope Eternyti's bunch doesn't discover the note. But anyway, how are we going to do this? We have two weeks."

Evolet ran his hand through his hair perplexedly. "Yeah, and Michael just keeps getting worse. Jaz, are you sure we shouldn't just let Eternyti give him her cure thing? It might save him—"

"No." Jasmine's voice was decisive. "It will kill him, I'm sure. He can't handle something like what Mom and Dad have right now. It's not just weakness, Evolet—I read the side effects, and—oh, I can't explain now. You can read them later. But we can't let her give Schwann3 to anyone else."

"Okay, then." Still running his hand through his hair, Evolet reflected grimly that he was in danger of becoming bald if this kind of heavy thinking continued to be necessary. "So what do we do?"

"You're the eldest one around now." She shrugged. "You figure that out."

"Oh, come on, Jaz—blast!" Evolet's patience snapped, as did a strand or two of hair when he jerked his hand away from his head suddenly. He stood up. "I'm going to scout out, then," he decided stonily.

She nodded. "Go do that. Michael should be safe here," she added, standing up as well. "I'm going to get some supplies."

Evolet merely grunted, stooping as the cave roof got lower and lower around the corner before the exit. Jasmine waited a moment longer to write a note for Michael, who might be disturbed if he woke up to find himself alone.

Meanwhile Evolet was sprinting away from the cave, back the five miles or so to the Eternity Labs premises. He pushed himself to the limit, and when he got to the heavy fence thirty minutes later, he was panting and red-faced.

He climbed the fence again, ignoring that at this time of the day the metal was getting scorchingly hot. Careful to avoid touching the electric current, he made his way to the top. Wiping the sweat off his face with one hand—a movement which reminded him he'd forgotten to bandage the gunshot wound—he held on between the barbs on the wire with the other, and peered out across the property.

The laboratory was obviously calming down after the excitement, and none of the guards that were quickly disappearing inside noticed the young man clinging to the fence. Ignoring them, Evolet counted eight buildings, all of them large, though a few were low-roofed. Then he saw a small crowd in the distance, and strained his eyes. It was a group of security guards, who were carrying a litter. He figured it must be his uncle Jason.

He watched them carry Jason to another building, which was, oddly enough, surrounded with seemingly random stakes sticking out of the ground and over eight feet high. The small procession stopped between two of them that were closer together than the others, and someone pulled out a card from their pocket.

They slid it across some kind of sensor on one of the posts, and Evolet saw something flash green. Then they kept going, into the building.

He sighed. Now he knew where they were keeping the other superhumans—but there had to be a catch. What were the posts there for?

* * *

Two hours later found Evolet finishing a complete route around the laboratory grounds, a very long and painstaking process. He could have just run, but he preferred to be up on the fence for now. It was definitely a good workout for him, even if—especially if—his clothes weren't as complete and nice-looking as they might have been that morning. He was covered in sweat, and his face was red and steamy as well as smeared with dirt. But he was satisfied with what he'd seen.

He lowered himself down slowly, gripping the top of the fence with both hands as his feet dangled four feet above the ground.

He dropped easily and on his feet—running back to the cave and Michael and Jasmine. He already had the beginning of a plan.

twenty-three

"Oh, *now* you unmute your phone. Evolet Whyte, I've been trying to call you for the last hour or so. What's going on?"

Moira sounded incredibly annoyed, but she smiled as she listened to Evolet's answer.

"Aunt Moira, I'm sorry! But so much has been happening, and—Jaz and I are on the way home. With Michael."

"And Jason? And what about your other siblings?" Moira shook her head in despair, though Evolet couldn't see her. "Evy, even if Jasmine is your favorite sister, you can't just keep leaving the other Whytes in random places and situations—"

"Moira, Ali is an adult! And I can't get them out now anyway. It's complicated—"

"—And we'll explain once we get there," came Jasmine's voice, interrupting her older brother's.

"I—" Moira blanked out momentarily.

"Aunt Moira, I know I'm a horrible nephew and you're going to beat me when I get back, but can we please have dinner when we do?" Evolet pleaded. Moira detected something desperate in his voice. "I have not eaten literally all day."

"Shut up, you had a bagel at the gas station," Jasmine interrupted him.

"Dinner?" Moira ignored Jasmine, as she figured Evolet was probably doing. She glanced at the clock, seeing that it was ten o'clock in the evening. "What time are you getting back?"

"Oh, about six PM tomorrow if we drive all night and day," she heard Evolet mumble.

"Evolet Whyte!" forty-five-year-old Moira gasped in horror and shock.

"It's an emergency—" he began weakly.

"—And we'll take it in shifts," came Jasmine's voice again, reassuringly. "Aunt Moira, can you please pick up Mom and Dad from the hospital tomorrow and bring them home? We need to talk to them, too."

Dazedly Moira shook her head. "Okay, I'll do that. But really—"

"See you tomorrow," Evolet interjected, hanging up.

Moira began to say about five other sentences, but broke off halfway through the first word of each one. She shook her head in disbelief.

"Idiots!"

But then she smiled. She could remember being like that once, too. And she knew that whatever Evolet and Jasmine were up to now, she was going to have to help them.

* * *

Meanwhile, Jason was waking up. He found himself in a small, white room with a bed, a table with a couple of books on it, and two doors. The floor, the walls, and even the ceiling were made of pure white tile, and he smiled grimly as he got up, rubbing his head to ease the quickly disappearing headache. He tested the first door. As he'd expected, it wouldn't open.

He jerked it hard, and then harder, testing it. Not the type that would be easy to break down.

But the other door opened, and he discovered a small restroom. Obviously he was meant to be staying in these rooms for some time.

He sighed, going back into the main room and sitting down on the bed. He felt in his pockets for his phone, and found it, but there was no signal here. Shrugging, he sat back, and shut his eyes, trying to remember how he'd gotten here.

They'd been talking to Eternyti. And then suddenly he'd gotten quite drowsy, and fallen asleep. Why—?

Of course! He groaned softly, and hit his forehead. The coffee!

Jason shook his head in disgust at his own naïvety, and sighed. Well, he was in here for good now, it seemed. But what about Evolet, and Jasmine, and Michael?

Suddenly he spotted a piece of paper sticking out of his shoe, and he grabbed it. His gray eyes flitted over it quickly, then again. He frowned.

Uncle Jason, Sorry to leave you here but we'll be back. See if you can contact the others. See you, Jasmine.

Slowly Jason began shaking his head. The note looked real enough. It was Jasmine's brief, to-the-point style, and her handwriting as well. But it made...too much sense.

A small smile played over his face as he struggled with the mental dilemma. It made sense for Jasmine to write it. Everything made perfect sense. Which would have been a good thing in any other circumstance, but—

Finally the twenty-five-year-old shrugged. It was all stuff he would've done anyway. But he would be careful.

He tore the note to pieces, dropping them on the floor. His gaze drifted upwards, and then he stood up and glanced around sharply, searching for anything that could be a camera. Then he saw it: a small black box in the top right corner. With a grim smile on his face, Jason climbed up on the table and tore the box out of the wall. There. Now he was really alone.

Quickly he rummaged through the room for anything he could use as a weapon or tool. The bed frame was metal, and he kept that in mind, especially when he looked through everything else and found nothing of use. So quietly he dumped the mattress on the floor, and proceeded to tackle the bed frame to loosen a rod or so, discovering in the meantime that they were very tightly fastened.

Finally one came loose after a valiant struggle, and Jason fell over backwards on the floor, holding the rod and looking just as satisfied with himself as Michael had earlier. Jason had espied some openings that looked like filters up near the ceiling, and now he shoved the bed frame up against the wall, almost like a ladder, and climbed it. It was a precarious attempt, as he had to hold the rod as well, but Jason seemed to have no trouble and soon found himself crouched between the top of the frame and the ceiling.

They were filters, he decided; and promptly shoved the rod through the nearest one. There was a tearing sound of plastic and metal, but Jason's muscles and rod won the battle, and the rod shoved through. He jerked it back, leaving himself with a peephole into the next room.

"Hello?" came a young, tremulous voice.

Jason's face broke into a giant grin. "Hey, Charles, this is your uncle. Can you do me a favor, pal, and dispose of the camera in there?"

"Done that ages ago," Charles Whyte returned. There was the sound of something heavy being moved, and then suddenly his boyish face popped into view.

Jason started, then grinned even harder, if that was possible. "Good, good." He noted happily that Charles's bright face, wreathed in light curly blond hair, looked healthy and in the best of spirits, though he was growing a beard, perhaps the first in his life.

The fifteen-year-old's dark blue eyes sparkled mischievously as he gestured helplessly towards his face. "No razor. Tragic!"

"Definitely." Jason paled. He'd never had a beard before, either, and he didn't want one.

Charles shrugged. "Anyway. How'd you get in here?"

"Can explain that later," Jason told him vaguely. "Do you know where everyone else is?"

"Ali's over there," Charles gestured across his room. "We've been communicating via knocks and kicks and Morse code. Primitive, maybe, but it does the trick. But if you're going to go tearing up the air filters—"

"It was a trial," Jason explained hastily. "Good. So I bet everyone is in this building."

"Oh, we are," Charles assured him. "What, did you get taken in unconscious or something?"

Jason nodded grimly. "Exactly. So you'll have to do some describing. And we need to pass the word: we'll be getting out of here soon."

Charles's eyebrows shot up. "Uncle Jason, I literally used my bed to ram the walls and door. I smashed up the tiles a bit, but there's something behind it all that won't give way."

"Well, I'll try," Jason shrugged. "I'm stronger than you, after all," he reminded his youngest nephew, grinning.

Charles took the jibe in good humor. "Well, then, good luck." He grinned back. "And I mean it."

twenty-four

"Siberia, Mongolia...Mexico. That's all I can think of." Evolet counted off the places on his fingers. "So there, I guess, or anywhere else, really, as long as it's out of the country and easy to—er—um—"

"Hide in," Jasmine finished for him calmly.

"Well, I mean, Mexico is closest," Moira pointed out dryly.

She, Evolet, Jasmine, Violet, and Conner Whyte were sitting around the dinner table at Moira's house, discussing plans urgently and quietly. Violet was out of the wheelchair, thankfully, but she and Conner still looked very old and tired, and so they weren't taking much of a part in the conversation.

Moira would be driving, anyway. Evolet and Jasmine had asked her to get Violet and Conner somewhere out of the country and find a place where all of them could stay.

And Michael was sitting on a chair in the corner of the room, the hood of his jacket drooping down over his face and his feet pulled up onto the chair. Evolet had tried to get him involved at first, but it was too much of an effort for the twelve-year-old, and Evolet had given up.

"Okay, well then, that works." Evolet shrugged, then seemed to remember something. "Oh, and Aunt Moira, I was going to ask—"

He stopped short, staring across the table at Jasmine, who was gesturing furiously at him. Confused, Evolet mouthed, "Huh?"

"Yes?" Moira's eyebrows shot up as her nephew didn't continue.

"I was just—er—wondering if I could—um—"

Moira sighed in impatience. "Evolet Whyte, just say it. Or I'm going to have words with your English teacher."

Evolet mouthed something else at Jasmine, and gave up. "Can I please borrow your motorcycle for—*oww!*"

"Aunt Moira, what Evolet wants to say is, can *we* please borrow your motorcycle to attack Eternity Labs?" Jasmine requested smoothly, meeting Evolet's speechless glare of fury with a small, innocent smile. She'd kicked him, and hard.

Moira's eyebrows shot up even higher than they already were. "That's my motorcycle you're talking about—"

"We'll be very extremely careful, I promise," Evolet broke in weakly, rubbing his shin ruefully.

"No scratches, dents, or explosions?" Moira went on, watching him like a hawk.

"I—I'll do my best," the twenty-year-old assured her eagerly. "And this way it'll go to Mexico, too. I mean, I hope—"

"It had better," Moira interrupted cleanly, standing up. "Anyway, to bed with everyone, including that poor child in the corner. You're not in trouble, Michael," she told him for what was probably the tenth time. "Oh, Evy, can you do the dishes? Wait, do you three have to leave now or—"

Evolet shook his head emphatically. "No. Tomorrow. And tomorrow I want to sleep in, please?"

Moira shrugged. "Why are you asking me?"

"I mean, if the police show up asking for me or anything, can you please tell them I need to sleep in after beating up a bunch of laboratory guards—no, you can't tell them that, it was a police summons—*bother!*" Evolet realized with a groan. He stood up as well. "Never mind. I'll just do the dishes."

"'Night, Evy," Jasmine grinned at him.

"'Night," he mumbled back, then glanced at his parents and forced a smile, though he hated to see them like this. "Goodnight, Mom, Dad." They smiled at him.

"Goodnight, Aunt Moira," Evolet went on, grabbing a pile of empty, dirty dishes and heading into the dark and dismal kitchen.

Moira followed him, flicking on the lights. "You aren't going to bed yet, sir—"

"I know," he assured her hastily, carefully putting the dishes down in the sink. He turned the water on.

His aunt started putting leftovers into the fridge. There was silence for a few minutes while Evolet scrubbed away industriously, but then Moira spoke up.

"You'll be careful?"

"Of course I'll be careful." Evolet gasped in shock that she would ask such a thing. "What about you? You're driving across the country—"

"I don't have a knack for getting into trouble like you do," Moira broke in sharply, "and I'm worried about you, Evolet. Don't do anything stupid."

"Do I ever?" he demanded indignantly.

"Yes," she returned without hesitation. "Evy, sometimes I wonder how you'll ever learn *any* responsibility—without Jasmine. But you need to look out for yourself, too, you know."

"I know." He nodded simply.

"Evolet, what are you going to do with your life?" she asked him suddenly.

He froze momentarily. "I—"

"Life isn't always exciting like it is now," she told him quietly. "Your parents know that, and so do I. You should settle down. Not now, of course, but you need to think about what you're going to do with your future."

"But I thought about that ages ago," Evolet protested. "I'm going to finish college, and then—"

"Not *that* kind of future!"

Moira shook her head vehemently.

"You need to find where you belong, Evolet. You're in this world for a reason, and rest assured, it is *not* shooting bad guys!"

Evolet's mind blanked temporarily, and he said the only thing he could think of. "I—it's not?"

"NO!" Moira shouted in exasperation. "Evolet Whyte—"

"I know, I know," he broke in desperately.

"No, you don't know, Evolet." Moira shook her head in disgust. "You don't understand. You have an obligation to do something with your life. And ever since I lost you, you've been jumping from one adventure to another." She could have added "literally," but she wasn't in the mood for that right now.

Evolet tensed. "Aunt Moira, you didn't lose me."

"Yes, I did," she contradicted him, turning away so that her nephew couldn't see her face. Her voice somehow got quieter than it already was. "I lost you five years ago, Evolet Whyte."

"But Aunt Moira, you don't understand," Evolet answered quietly, putting down the dish he was holding. "I'm still Evolet. I'm still Evy."

"Not the Evy you once were." Moira shook her head. "You were *my* Evy."

"But I still am," Evolet insisted.

She put the dish she'd been holding in the fridge, and came back for another. Taking a plate off the counter close to Evolet and the sink, she scraped it into a container. "You've changed."

"So have you," he noted stubbornly, glancing at her in the dim kitchen light. He winced when he saw her graying hair, once a beautiful light brown but now interspersed with gray. But he liked the gray—better, in fact.

She didn't answer, and suddenly he realized she was fighting tears. He winced again and stopped washing the dishes.

"I'm sorry for being a crazy, hard-to-deal-with nephew," he whispered, touching her arm lightly.

Suddenly she turned and wrapped her arms around him in a crushing bear hug. "Promise me you'll come back safe, Evolet," she told him, her voice thick with meaning.

"I promise," he murmured back, his voice cracking as his own eyes misted. "I'll meet you and Mom and Dad—safely in Mexico. I promise."

twenty-five

About a week later, Evolet, Jasmine, and Michael were back at their cave in Texas, discussing final plans.

They sat in a circle at the widest part of the cave, Jasmine with her laptop on her lap and Evolet with a notebook open to a rough sketch of the laboratory layout. Michael sat precariously on one of the broken-off rocky columns nearby, his feet dangling.

All of their faces were serious, though Evolet tried to maintain a cheerful grin.

"But even if it's lasers, we just have to put out the electricity and they won't work, right?" he was asking Jasmine. "Or did your scanner pick up something that would invalidate that suggestion?"

The eighteen-year-old shook her head slowly. "No, it didn't. Or it hasn't yet. But how to get to the power supply, that's another question."

"Well, where is it?" Michael asked curiously.

"The main power source is eight feet below ground in that very same building which is surrounded by the laser fence," she informed the two matter-of-factly, her light blue eyes grim.

Evolet nodded as a matter of course, while the information took a moment to register. "Mhmm. That's actually...pretty smart," he admitted weakly.

"So there goes that idea," Michael muttered. He sighed, staring up at the roof of the cave.

"But we could still get ahold of an ID card somehow, I bet," Evolet added brightly. "Right, Jaz?"

"I guess," she admitted begrudgingly. "We'll do that, then. What next?"

"What next?" Evolet repeated, gaining momentum. His eyes sparkled with enthusiasm, and he leaned forward towards Jasmine and Michael excitedly. "I'll tell you what's next. Listen up!"

* * *

"The gate is completely secured? Good. And the main fence still only at 7,000 volts? Good as well. Any news from the lab, Dr. Schwann?"

The speaker was Major Lucius Arcilla, Eternyti's military acquaintance who was just as eager as she was to rid the world of the T4 threat. He had come to personally supervise the Eternity Labs' defense for the coming crisis.

Eternyti had her own business to attend to: getting more Schwann3 ready, a week ahead of time.

She was nearly finished, but she'd taken the time out to attend this final conference before what they figured would be the attack night. They'd released a statement to the press that the cure would be ready sometime the next day—so the Whytes would have no choice but to attack that night if they wanted to prevent the others from getting the cure.

Not like they would succeed, anyway.

"Five hours on the timer," the young scientist told Lucius, glancing down at her watch. She smiled. "It'll be ready few minutes after one, I think."

"Good." Lucius nodded his approval. "What about Containment?"

Eternyti openly hesitated, but only for a moment. "The cameras are long gone, but we can tell that they've made contact with each other. But they haven't tried to break out yet."

"Also good." Lucius smiled affably. "But they'll be kept contained till injection time?"

"Oh, yes." Eternyti laughed confidently. "There's no way they can get through the laser fence. And if they try—well, that's their problem."

Lucius laughed as well. "Good, then. I think we're ready."

"Then I'll be off to the lab," Eternyti returned, standing up from her chair at the meeting room table. "I'll leave you to your officers. Cure before two—I promise!"

She left the room, made her way briskly down the hallway, and exited the building. As she stepped lightly across the grassy space between this building and the next, she kept looking around her, and suddenly became aware of a brief flash of light over by the boundary fence.

She stopped short, watching where she'd seen it.

A moment later there was just the tiniest reflection of light, some distance above the first flash, but it was enough for her.

Eternyti hurried on her way, but pulled a small radio out of her pocket and spoke into it quietly and swiftly.

"They're heading in."

* * *

"Dangerous, high, electrified, barbed-wired, uhh..." Evolet mumbled away to himself as he and the others approached Eternity Labs at an easy, cautious pace.

"What are you doing?" Jasmine hissed. "We're supposed to be making no noise."

"I'm just giving myself the reasons not to climb that thing again," he muttered.

He saw a look of disbelief flash across her face through the dimming evening twilight. "Evy—shut up. You're climbing it anyway."

"I know," he told himself mournfully.

"Well then, sh—"

"Wonder what'll happen if I touch the fence and touch the ground at the same time," Michael remarked under his breath, looking up at the somewhat imposing structure and then down at his shoes while a smirk stole over his face.

"Uhh...you could try it, but *I* wouldn't," Jasmine muttered, shaking her head in despair. "I mean, that's thousands of volts right there." She gestured towards the fence, which was now only a few feet away from them.

Michael nodded, his smile fading somewhat. "Maybe I won't try it then."

They stopped, glancing up and around.

The boundary fence seemed normal, and there weren't any guards around. There were some in the distance, visible by means of the huge searchlights that lit the spaces in between buildings, but not close enough to notice the intruders.

"Everyone got gloves?" Evolet asked quietly. "Yes? Well then. Let's get going. But, whatever you do, don't touch the fence with your bare skin. It could be at the same strength it was last time—or it could be more. We don't know."

"Got it." Jasmine nodded briefly. "No more speeches—let's go."

twenty-six

Some distance away, in the main laboratory building, while Eternyti was finishing up the second batch of Schwann3 in the underground portion of the Containment Facility, another young scientist was working on a project of her own. The name on her badge read *Scarlet Dawes*.

She was walking quickly down a deserted hall, casting occasional glances over her shoulder as if she were afraid of being followed, and carrying a small box of supplies. She looked like she was twenty, or maybe even younger; her eyes were blue, speckled with coral; her hair was a deep, straight red. On the left side of her face there was a section of her hair that was completely white, though only the top inch or so was. It looked like she'd been wearing a hood to cover it, but the hood had fallen back, and her hands were full with the box. So she contented herself with hurrying.

Finally she reached what appeared to be her destination: a door labeled *Experimentals.*

Scarlet balanced the box with one hand—it looked heavy, but she held it easily—and scanned her ID with the other. The door opened for her, and she stepped into the room, looking around and breathing a sigh of relief that the room was dark and empty. As the door shut again behind her, she put the box down on a long table and flicked a switch on the wall. The room lit up, and there was a stirring from the covered cages at the far end of the room.

Scarlet hurried over to a corner and pushed aside a section of the tarp, revealing stacked cages of small, white laboratory mice. She bent down to a couple of cages on the bottom row, and glanced in at the first one. Her face fell.

"Both dead," she whispered aloud to herself. "It didn't work. Stabilizer A—not working." She said it like she was making a mental note. Which indeed she was.

Then she glanced into the second one, and as her face came into view two white mice scuttled away in a fright. Scarlet fairly beamed.

"You're alive!" she murmured in relief, unlatching the cage door. She reached into the cage, pulling out one of the mice, which seemed eager to escape her gloved hand. It might be said in the mouse's defense that Scarlet's hand was unusually warm—running a temperature, in fact. But she held the creature firmly, and took it out of the cage, shutting the door on its roommate and taking the mouse she'd selected over to a small box inset in the side wall.

Dropping the animal carefully into the box, she turned on a screen display on the side of the machine, and waited for results. They came in a matter of seconds, as a small red laser light played over the mouse in the box.

"Normal temperature," Scarlet observed, mumbling to herself. Her voice growing more excited as she read. "Normal weight. Vitals fully functioning. I think I have it!"

She retrieved the mouse, which was none the worse for its ordeal in the box. Taking it over to the table where she'd left her box of supplies, Scarlet put it down gently and cupped her right hand over it firmly while she opened the box and pulled out four test strips and lancets with her left. She proceeded to draw blood from the small animal, which wriggled in her hand but otherwise didn't react.

Scarlet was so jubilant. For the past few days, that mouse—and the other three—had been completely rabid after she'd injected them with T6. And yesterday Scarlet had given them two different chemical solutions. It seemed that the mice had survived only Solution B.

Now Scarlet ran the T4, T5, hyper-T5, and T6 tests, and held the mouse impatiently while she waited for these results, which took considerably longer—fifteen minutes. She grew considerably more anxious that someone might come into the room...and addressed her anxiety by locking the door with her ID. Then she could relax.

Finally the timer went off. Scarlet had been pacing, talking softly to the mouse; now she bolted over to where she'd left the timer, even flipping across a table in her haste, the mouse still safe in one hand. It took her only a couple of seconds to look over the tests, and then about thirty more to fully register the results.

T4 was faint. T5 was more pronounced. T6 was as faint as T4. But hyper-T5 was bold and clear.

"T5," Scarlet whispered to herself. "Hyper-T5. Pure Hyper-T5!"

And while she gaped in happy surprise, the mouse decided it was tired of being held in an overly warm hand, even if that hand was covered in a glove. Suddenly rearing, it headbutted the side of her hand, slamming its extra-sharp, hyper-T5 teeth through the glove and into her hand.

"OWW!" Scarlet wrung her hand, shocked by the sudden pain, and accidentally threw the mouse across the room. She drew breath in quickly, and tore the glove off her hand to reveal a quickly bleeding cut.

Scarlet literally flew across the room to a sink, though the pain was already disappearing, and washed her hands thoroughly with disinfectant. Disinfectant that didn't sting her as much as it might have a normal person, but she knew that was because she had been injected with T6 for about a week now. She'd done that herself.

Now she went to look for the mouse and get it back into the cage, armed with fresh gloves. She got it cornered and safely into a small cardboard box before she realized her temperature was dropping.

"Oh, twisty tornadoes!" she shouted in annoyance, rushing the mouse back over to the cage and dumping it in unceremoniously, then clapping her hand to her forehead, wincing when she realized it was cooler than it usually was.

Something crossed her mind, and she ran over to her box of tests, pulling out another strip for hyper-T5.

But suddenly she started feeling overwhelmingly weak, and she collapsed into a chair, the test strip falling from her fingers.

She gasped for air, her head falling back. She felt increasingly faint and lightheaded, but gradually she became aware that the bite didn't hurt anymore. In fact, nothing hurt.

It took a moment for that to register. *Nothing* hurt. There wasn't even the dull, pressing fire of the T6 that she'd gotten somewhat used to in the past few days.

She stood up, her hands trembling. She stared at them, willing them to be still. It took about half a minute, but then they were still. The dizzy feeling was going away, leaving behind a feeling of strength, power, and painlessness.

Scarlet made her way over to some equipment racks at the other end of the room near the sinks, her steps growing stronger and stronger as she walked. By the time she got there she felt completely herself—and more. She found a thermometer and took her own temperature.

97.6°. Completely normal and healthy.

Her blue eyes lit up, and if she'd looked in a mirror, she would've noticed that the coral coloring was completely gone. She went back and grabbed the test strip she'd dropped. Her fingers were now sure and steady, and she took a lancet and tested herself fearlessly.

No timer had ever passed so slowly. Scarlet spent the time cleaning up after herself, replacing the thermometer and disposing of the test strips from the mouse. She also took her second compound, a large vial of pale blue liquid, out of the box.

She looked at it a moment before putting it back with a muttered comment that she wasn't thinking straight yet. Taking out the first compound, the one that had killed the mice, she wrapped it in a couple of red trash bags and disposed of it in a trash can marked *Biohazard*.

Snatching up her box and test strip, she made for the door, after ensuring that her hood was up and the room looked completely normal. That done, she unlocked the door and left the room, brushing by another scientist as she marched swiftly—nearly ran—down the hall with the box and test strip, heading for her personal office.

She tensed as an announcement blared in the hallway. "Infiltration Alert— breach in west boundary fence. Military, please report to your posts. Civilians, please report to lodgings or to shelter. Infiltration Alert—breach..."

"Nah," she answered it under her breath, an entirely useless step but one she took anyway, feeling slightly reckless. "I have a *lot* to do tonight."

With that in mind, she fairly tore along the hall. No one noticed her because they were all rushing as well. Scarlet ducked discreetly into her office, locked the door behind her, and nearly smashed her phone as the fifteen-minute timer went off. She had smashed a phone the other day, after she'd given herself T6. But she didn't intend to let that happen again.

Scarlet shut her eyes for a moment and forced herself to take a deep breath before she looked at the test strip. When she did, she breathed an immense sigh of relief.

"Hyper-T5... It *works!*"

She collapsed into her desk chair, suddenly bursting into almost maniacal nervous laughter. Finally she got up.

"It works!" she whispered to herself again, taking the rest of the compound that had worked out of the box and running it over to a small syringe-filling machine that she'd smuggled into her office earlier. She emptied most of the large vial into the canister, closed both the vial and the canister quickly, and hit a button on the machine, selecting the number *8*.

Then she left the vial on her desk and threw open a filing cabinet drawer, rummaging through the folders in it till she found one labeled Dawes: *T6S-2*. She pulled that one out and provided herself with a leather folder-case large enough to hold the paper-filled folder and the large vial.

Having zipped it closed most of the way, Scarlet glanced across the small office to the machine.

"Four minutes left," she murmured. "Well, we'll see what happens. Oh my. I can't believe it worked!"

twenty-seven

After the three attackers crossed the boundary fence together, unimpeded by any guards—much to their surprise—they split up and went their respective ways.

Evolet was to head to the main laboratory building, find the where Schwann3 was being produced, and destroy it; Jasmine and Michael would free those in containment.

Michael seemed unusually cheerful and excited as he and Jasmine snuck over to a building to see if they could borrow someone's identity tag. Jasmine kept her eyes on him. He seemed to be okay.

"Hang on," she whispered to him, suddenly increasing speed and dashing forward towards the side of a building. She knocked over a laboratory security guard almost effortlessly, rendering him unconscious in the process, and grabbed his ID card.

By that time, Michael had caught up with her, and together they made their way swiftly over to the Containment Facility, their dark clothes and confident air helping camouflage them.

They got there a few minutes later, waiting for an opportune moment to flash the ID and slip past the laser fence. For some reason the grounds were fairly deserted—though Jasmine was sure the laboratory officials would've been alerted by now—and that opportune moment came quickly.

Everything went like clockwork, and soon they found themselves inside. Jasmine breathed a sigh of relief that no one seemed to have noticed them.

She probably wouldn't have been so relieved had she known about the sentry posted just outside the building entrance, discreetly hidden around a corner. Now he lifted a walkie-talkie to his mouth and spoke into it softly.

"Targets 2 and 3 have entered the building. Awaiting orders."

* * *

"Targets 2 and 3 have entered the building. Awaiting orders."

Major Lucius Arcilla smiled grimly as he listened. Quickly, he made a reply, not to the guard who'd spoken, but to another section of the laboratory security setup.

"Initiate Plan A. But Target 1 is still outside the net."

* * *

"Something's happening," Jason told Charles, and the word was passed along the line.

The twenty-five-year-old was lying ear-down on the tile floor, listening carefully. The building was quieter than it usually was, but his keener-than-usual ears picked up some sounds nonetheless.

An alarm was going off—an lockdown. Some people were talking quickly and quietly; now they walked out of hearing range. But what Jason was listening for was there as well: a constant beeping sound that had begun only a few hours ago. Frowning, he stood up.

"Charles, something tells me that they've got Schwann3 in the final stages. Is everyone ready to get out of here?"

"Yeah, we all are," came his nephew's cheery reply from next door. "'Cept the six kids, of course."

"You're a kid, you know," Jason observed thoughtfully.

"Yeah, I know, but not a *kid* kid," Charles muttered to himself. "When do we break out?"

Jason glanced at his watch and shrugged helplessly.

"Alert went out two minutes ago. How about we give it another three?"

* * *

"This place is big, remember," Jasmine whispered to Michael once they got fairly inside the building. "Split up to find them? You head upstairs and I'll tackle below."

He nodded. "Fine with me."

"And be careful about using your paradraline," she warned him. "You may well need to be fighting fit for this."

Michael felt in his pocket for the vials he always carried with him now—a solution that slowed down his blood flow to make the T6 effects less effective mentally as well as physically.

"Right," he replied briskly. "See you soon."

Jasmine gave him a little wave, then marched off towards where she'd seen elevators going down. She selected an empty one and took it down to the next floor.

There, the doors locked, and a warning flashed on the screen.

DNA Confirmation Required.

"DNA?" the Whyte girl wondered aloud, glancing at the ID—really glancing at it—for the first time. She had a sinking feeling that her DNA wasn't going to be anything like that of the middle-aged man pictured on the card. "No matter!"

Looking up, she jumped and pulled down a ceiling panel that was already loose. She tossed it aside and inspected the mess of wires now visible.

After thinking hard for a moment, Jasmine selected the biggest red cord and jerked it. Sparks scattered, the elevator control display flashed, and suddenly the doors began jerking open.

Jasmine grinned. "Lucky!"

A moment later she peered out into the hallway. It seemed empty, but it was short, with only one other door at the end, a heavily secured one. Shrugging, Jasmine marched directly up to it and inserted her ID. She frowned when it asked her for a finger combination password.

"No clue," she murmured—and stared at the panel itself. Some places were more heavily smudged than the rest. Jasmine's fingers moved rapidly as she connected them.

After a few red flashes, it seemed she got the correct combination, and the door slid open. Jasmine pressed herself against the wall for a few seconds in case someone was already in the room.

It was dark, and only a few lights were on in the far corner, where a tall, red-haired scientist stood alone and watched the countdown on a display.

Eternyti looked up as Jasmine stepped silently into the room and the door slid shut behind her.

"Jasmine Whyte," Eternyti observed, her voice quiet. "How'd *you* get in here?"

twenty-eight

"It doesn't matter," Jasmine shrugged, shaking her head as Eternyti suddenly reached for an alert button. Flipping across the room, Jasmine covered the button with her hand just in time. "Let's not, okay? I don't wanna mess with security."

Eternyti stepped a couple of paces away from Jasmine, between her and the Schwann3 machine. Slowly she smiled. "Why are you doing this, Jasmine? Those kids aren't even related to you."

Jasmine smiled back, a trifle condescendingly. "T4 is thicker than water, Doctor Schwann."

Eternyti glanced behind her at the machine just long enough to check the timer. Two hours and nine minutes. Her eyes flashed angrily as she hit a red emergency button. The machine sped up.

The scientist glanced back at the younger Whyte girl. "Why are *you* here? I told you you'd have to prove this scientifically."

Jasmine shrugged. "I wasn't planning on meeting you. In fact, I'm looking for my uncle, and my sister, and my brother, and the rest of them. So if you'll just tell me—"

Eternyti shook her head furiously. "This isn't going to work, Jasmine. You can't win."

Suddenly she lunged forward, pulling an uncapped syringe out of her pocket and aiming for Jasmine's unprotected neck. Jasmine was startled, but she swayed away just in time, at the same moment as she kicked Eternyti's syringe away. The vial clattered away on the tile floor without breaking, and Eternyti chased after it.

Jasmine was about to follow her, but suddenly her gaze fell on the machine Eternyti had been standing in front of, and she tensed.

3.54.

3.53.

"Schwann3," Jasmine breathed as the realization hit her. Schwann3, with less than four minutes left on the timer!

She stepped over to the machine, wondering what was going on inside it. She wondered for only a split half-second before she lifted her hand and touched the display gently, looking for the cancel button, and—more importantly—gauging how hard she would have to smash the thing against the wall to destroy it and its contents completely.

But before she grabbed the machine, Eternyti pounced on her from behind, bringing Jasmine to the ground with a surprisingly strong effort.

Jasmine landed on her back, but kicked at the base of the machine, accidentally launching herself across the room—and slamming her head into the opposite wall. She was dazed for a moment, and Eternyti took advantage of that to initiate an emergency sequence. The Schwann3 machine slid into a slot in the wall, and a metal plate closed over it, adding extra protection.

As Jasmine got quickly to her feet, Eternyti pulled out a handgun and started shooting rapidly in an effort to keep Jasmine at the other side of the room. Most of the bullets fell harmlessly when they hit her purple jacket, but a couple of them were headed in another direction, and Jasmine winced as one grazed her cheek and another clipped through the glove on her right hand.

Then Eternyti's gun ran out of bullets, and when Jasmine hesitantly began to approach, Eternyti threw the firearm at her, without a touch of hesitation on her part. Jasmine caught it, smiled distractedly at Eternyti, and shoved the scientist out of the way with her bleeding hand. With the other, she hurled the gun at the metal panel covering the Schwann3 machine. The panel shook under the impact and was dented.

Jasmine bit her lip, realizing that the panel was built especially to withstand something like that. She looked around the room desperately for something else she could use—

"Miss Whyte, I suggest you surrender now," came Eternyti's voice behind her.

Jasmine ignored the scientist just as much as she ignored her cut hand and cheek, digging through a drawerful of dissection tools.

"Busy," she mumbled, selecting a small knife that looked sharp. She turned to face the panel again.

Just in time to dodge Eternyti's throwing a small, purple-tinted crystal knife at Jasmine's neck. As it was, she didn't avoid it completely; the knife landed in her shoulder.

Jasmine froze, drawing breath in sharply. The blade had gone right through the purple jacket, and her shoulder was bleeding now. Even T4 couldn't deal with it that fast.

She turned to look at Eternyti, who was smiling slightly. Jasmine sat down on the table behind her, grabbing her shoulder with her already injured hand and exerting pressure as well as covering the wound with her glove.

"Where'd you get that?" she hissed at Eternyti. "That was Louis's."

"It doesn't matter," Eternyti told her, smugly copying Jasmine's response from only a few minutes before.

Jasmine shook her head slowly. "You're going to have to let me stop that machine, Doctor Schwann. At least, I assume that your theory of disproving theories is in self-defense?"

She didn't bother to speak clearly, being slightly distracted, and Eternyti was momentarily confused. "No?"

"No?" Jasmine repeated, glancing at the plain metal knife in her other hand before she took a deep breath.

Swiping it across the bloodiest part of her jacket, she looked at Eternyti again with just a hint of a smile on her face.

"No?" she returned once more. "Well, this is."

With that, she threw the knife accurately and swiftly at Eternyti, who ducked the "contaminated" blade—but not quickly enough to avoid being hit in the arm.

It was only a slight cut, but the blood drained from Eternyti's face as she realized what Jasmine had done. Gasping, she stumbled back, bumping into a table and sitting down on it automatically.

With an effort, Jasmine clenched her teeth together and jerked the purple knife out of her shoulder, keeping her hand there to staunch the flow that was slowing gradually. She turned the knife over in her hands once before heading back over to the panel. It would suit her purposes even better than what she'd found.

Smiling satisfiedly, as well as ruefully, she sliced around the edges of the panel. It was slow going with one hand, but with Jasmine that was only as "slow" as the average person would be with both hands. She didn't even pause when she heard Eternyti's voice from where the older scientist sat halfway across the room, recovering—if one could call T4ification recovering.

"Leave it." Her voice was sharp and angry. "You don't know what you're doing."

"Do you feel like a virus?" Jasmine returned, her own voice just as angry. "Well, *do you?*"

"I said leave it," Eternyti snapped.

"Blow your top off somewhere else, please," Jasmine muttered, yanking the rest of the panel away from the wall.

She reached in for the machine, just as it beeped.

Solution Finished.

"Hang it," Jasmine whispered, hearing Eternyti behind her.

Maybe turning her into a "virus" had been a mistake, Jasmine reflected for a moment before she and Eternyti grabbed the machine—simultaneously.

They both held onto it, pulling their hardest.

"You stupid! Let go!" Eternyti shouted at her, but Jasmine had other methods, and smoothly she kicked high, knocking Eternyti's unused-to-being-superstrong hands off the machine.

She jerked it away, then gathered all her strength to throw it at the concrete wall. An action which occurred about 0.7 seconds later.

Jasmine grinned in spite of herself and her injuries as the metal cylinder smashed into the wall, breaking it and itself at the same time.

An enraged look of short-suffering impatience came over her face as she heard Eternyti suddenly start talking behind her, though not to her. "Major Arcilla, major emergency in Containment Lab 02. The cure is ready, but—"

"But you're a virus," Jasmine added, gleefully albeit annoyedly, and grabbed the radio from Eternyti, smashing it into the wall and grabbing hold of the untrained scientist a moment later. She pushed Eternyti up against the wall, her eyes flashing. "Now, I'm not kidding. What's the way out of here?"

She couldn't help but notice when Eternyti's eyes flitted momentarily over to a section of the laboratory wall.

Jasmine followed her gaze. There was a secret door there.

She grinned. "Thanks!"

twenty-nine

While Jasmine was fighting Eternyti for Schwann3, Evolet wasn't having much luck in locating the same objective.

He was just thankful that no one had taken the time to call him out yet for disobeying the lockdown order as he slipped down the halls in the main laboratory building, ducking into the various rooms as he went—at least, the ones that he could get into without some serious exertion.

About halfway down the hall, which was now empty, he stopped, shaking his head in despair.

"Where would they have it?" he asked himself dolefully. "What if—"

Suddenly a door slid open, and Evolet wheeled around to see a young scientist stepping out of her office, clutching a leather folder to her chest and looking around cautiously before her gaze lit on Evolet. She stared at him, and he stared back. She was tall, with a hood pulled over dark red hair. Her eyes were blue, and unusually confident as she took in Evolet and the situation.

But still he spoke first. "I can ask you politely to leave, or I could just tell you to get lost before I—er—"

She smiled slightly. "I'd rather not."

"I don't want to hurt you," Evolet went on, somewhat annoyed that she wouldn't just run. "And I have stuff to do here. So, really—"

"So do I," the redhead returned swiftly, her smile widening. "Do you want to get out of my way?"

Evolet was really perplexed now. "Who are you?" he demanded, glancing at the ID card pinned on her lapel even as he asked.

"My name's Scarlet. But anyway, this is for you," Scarlet added, suddenly seeming to remember what she was doing out in the hallway. She shoved the leather folder at him, her smile fading into a keen, blank business expression. "And it works."

"What?" Evolet asked, not taking it. "What is it?"

She made an impatient gesture. "It's T6 Stabilizer. You're Evolet Whyte," she added needlessly—Evolet already knew she knew who he was. "Anyway, like I said, it works."

Slowly he took it, still staring into her frank and open eyes. "Stabilizer?"

She nodded emphatically. "Yeah. That's what you guys need, isn't it? Or what Michael Leblanc and those other kids need?"

"I mean—" Evolet began, still staring.

Scarlet sighed.

"Look," she told him, pushing her hood back and pointing at a formerly hidden streak of white hair near the front of her face. "I'm one of Eternyti's scientists. Does that help? Probably not, but I gave myself T6 to try to find a real cure, since you guys didn't seem to like the first one. I came up with it, and...a mouse decided to test it on me," she explained, her face breaking into a grin.

Evolet was still confused, and he reached his free hand up to run it through his hair. "You're—"

"Superhuman," Scarlet finished for him. "But not T6 anymore—hyper-T5. I'm telling you that thing *works!*"

Evolet shook his head. "Miss Dawes, no offense, but I can't just use some random formula on those kids. That'd be worse than what Eternyti's trying to do."

With a sudden, strong movement that greatly hinted at her hyper-T5, Scarlet snatched the folder back with a look of annoyance. "Right, that's right, but—" She broke off, closing her eyes. Finally she opened them. "Okay. Then do you want me to get you into the Containment Building? Schwann3 isn't anywhere over here."

"I—it's not?" Evolet stammered. For some reason he was feeling completely out of his depth here.

"No, it's not," Scarlet replied hurriedly, tucking her folder under her arm and flouncing down the hallway, the way Evolet had come. "If you're coming, you'd better hurry up!"

* * *

Meanwhile, Michael had located a row of doubly locked doors. He tried them all nonetheless, and then, as he was alone, began to bang. He was rewarded with a muffled shout from inside the first room he tried. A voice that he didn't recognize, but it was something like Jasmine's.

"Who's there?"

"Mike," Michael shouted back excitedly. "Who are you?"

"Michael Leblanc? I'm Alison," came the answer. "Is it time to break out of here?"

"It is that," the boy returned, grinning although there was no one there to see him. "What, do you—"

"Stand away from the door," Alison ordered.

Michael jumped back just in time as the door came flying into the hallway and Alison followed it out.

Yes, she was Jasmine's twin, Michael realized: tall, agile, brown-haired and blue-eyed, with Violet Whyte's sharp chin. He grinned weakly at her.

"I have been dying to do that," she confided, stepping on the fallen door with a satisfied smirk and then marching over to the next. "Charles! Let's go!"

Michael watched, amazed and delighted, as the entire hallway-full of superhumans proceeded to break out of their respective prisons. Each one came armed, too—mostly with metal rods.

Michael counted them. Jason. Then Alison. The youngest Whyte, Charles. Some older woman he didn't know but seemed to be called Tina. And then Jason's two older siblings he'd never heard about.

The superhumans gathered in the hallway, conversing in low tones. Michael was somewhat hesitant to join them, but then Jason motioned him over with a grin, and he joined the circle.

"You and I can do it, Jason," Jason's older brother was telling him quietly.

"We can? Let's do it, then," Jason grinned optimistically, heading over to the other side of the hallway. "First things first. Who's in here?" he yelled suddenly, banging hard on the door.

"Who are you?" came a weak, frightened child's voice.

Michael recognized it, and his face broke into a smile as he realized what Jason and Petyr Foley were going to do. "It's Gregory! Jason, it's Gregory—"

"Gregory?" Petyr looked perplexed.

"Gregory Cruz, one of the kids Monet and Staunton kidnapped," Jason explained hurriedly. "Thanks, Mike. Come on, Petyr—let's get him out!"

thirty

"Richards, what is taking so long?" Major Lucius Arcilla demanded of one of his subordinates.

The Major's face was filled with annoyance and impatience. He had expected all of the superhumans to be contained by now and ready for Schwann3. But he hadn't yet been assured that the three attackers were actually inside the Containment Facility, which was rather essential to his plan.

The officer merely frowned. "It appears only two went to Containment, Major. The other—Whyte, Evolet Whyte—is, er—"

"Is where?" Lucius turned on him with a furious gesture.

Richards backed off slowly. "*Was* in the main building, Major."

"*Was?* What about *now?*" Lucius growled. "Eliminated?"

"No, actually," Richards stammered, "well, I mean, not that I know of—"

"Just answer the question!" the Major roared.

"We don't know, Major!" Richards admitted. "We're working on it."

Lucius fixed him with an incredulous look of disgust. "You seriously *lost* him? Never mind, I'll head out there myself. That's the only way to get anything done," he reflected grimly, throwing his rifle over his shoulder and heading for the door.

Richards breathed a sigh of relief, but it was too soon, and Lucius heard him. "And you can get out there, too!" Lucius shouted at him before he left the room.

He frowned deeply as he marched down the short hall and outside into the dark night. Lucius was only too aware that they had to capture all of the superhumans tonight and inject them with Schwann3. Later on, they could possibly contain them in lunatic asylums as well.

He knew full well that what Eternyti was doing with her experimental cure was quite illegal, and also that, by helping her, he was also going on the wrong side of the law. But Lucius fully believed in the precept that the end justifies the means, and he was also determined to eliminate superhumans entirely.

Maybe he didn't quite believe Eternyti's theory that they weren't truly human—but it wasn't rocket science to see that anyone who was superstrong could be a threat. The Major didn't have to be a historian to know that they very often had been, especially in recent years.

The trouble with superhumans was just getting worse. And although, except in the case of the Purple Blitzkrieg, it had been kept within the boundaries of the superhumans themselves, this latest flare with Ayan Monet and Louis Staunton had involved innocent civilians.

Yes, the trouble was only going to get worse, Lucius believed.

So that was why he was here—to finish this once and for all.

Smiling grimly, Lucius pulled out his walkie-talkie and held the PTT button. He wanted to talk to Eternyti—she'd hinted that there was a way to speed up the Schwann3 process, and Lucius was pretty sure that it was going to become necessary.

But she didn't answer.

His main radio—the one that connected with everyone's—gave off a warning—in Eternyti's voice.

"Major Arcilla, major emergency in Containment Lab 02. The cure is ready, but—"

And then it cut off, ending abruptly in an ear-shattering crash and burst of static. Lucius cringed.

"But what?" he asked in return, though he knew he wasn't going to get an answer. And he didn't.

Lucius sighed and shook his head. "Glenn, are you on the line?" he questioned for his second-in-command.

"Yes, I am, Major Arcilla," came a young woman's somewhat distracted voice.

"I'm going to take everyone in. Where are you now?"

"Downstairs." Glenn's voice was clearly hesitant. "Er, Major—"

"What now?" Lucius barked, closing his eyes in despair.

"Something you should know. There seems to be a T4 contamination in the Schwann3 laboratory," Glenn explained slowly.

"What?" Lucius frowned. "You mean—"

"I mean the laboratory has been wrecked—Doctor Schwann is trying to get the cure going again—and meanwhile the superhumans have broken loose upstairs." The words came faster and faster. "Major, can you please hurry with reinforcements? It's only a matter of minutes—"

"*What's* only a matter of minutes?" But Lucius was already on his way to the general alarm control room, located near the center of the Eternity Labs compound.

"Major, *they're coming.*" Glenn sounded strained. "Please hurry—"

"Glenn, I'll be right over."

Lucius had his hand on the alarm now.

"In the meantime—exterminate."

"Exterminate?" Glenn echoed dully. "But—"

"You heard me!" Lucius interrupted urgently. "Exterminate!"

* * *

In the Schwann3 laboratory, Glenn slowly replaced her walkie-talkie in her belt. She'd been called in to reinforce the security at Eternity Labs. Then she and the other Army soldiers had been issued with biohazard weapons and safety equipment. And now—*exterminate?*

But orders were orders. They always were with Glenn, and that was how she'd gotten to her current rank. And the other soldiers around had already heard the order anyway. So Glenn shrugged off the doubt and hopped down from the table she'd been sitting on.

"Exterminate," she announced needlessly, looking around.

Jasmine had left the laboratory a complete mess before heading back upstairs. Glenn's team had arrived shortly after that and found the place totaled, what with lights dangling from the ceiling, the wall smashed up in places, tables overturned, blood on the floor.

Eternyti had been—and still was—setting up the Schwann3 machine again. She hadn't spoken much—in fact, she hadn't said a word.

Glenn watched her for a few seconds and could see that the scientist's hands were trembling nervously. Clearly, she was shaken.

But who wouldn't be, after a face-off with a superhuman?

Sighing, Glenn went over to one of her soldiers, who was standing near the barricaded door. He was listening carefully, his ears to the panel. As Glenn approached, he straightened and glanced at her.

"Status?" she asked simply.

"They're coming downstairs," he whispered. "I'd say three minutes."

"Three minutes. Okay, then."

Glenn shrugged, pulling her handgun off her belt and checking to make sure it was loaded. Satisfied, she looked up and smiled at the soldier.

"And this is the only way out now," she went on, more to herself than to him. "We've got them."

* * *

"We can't go out the way we came in." Michael shook his head emphatically from where he was perched on Jason's shoulders, having been recruited to get up there and look out of a high window. "It's literally flooded with soldiers," he explained as the man lowered him to the floor easily.

Alison smiled grimly. "And how does that mean we can't go out that way?"

"They have Schwann2, LVK, and the like—that's how," came her twin sister's voice suddenly as Jasmine came jogging up a flight of stairs. "Hey, guys."

"Jaz—what happened to you?" Charles stared in frank amazement at his older sister.

Though Jasmine was smiling—a smile much like Alison's—there was a makeshift bandage on her shoulder, not to mention bloodstains around it on her purple jacket. Her cheek had been bleeding, though it seemed to be sealing up now, and her right glove was bloody. Besides that, her hair was slightly awry, and there was a light burning in her eyes that alerted those who knew her—Jasmine had gone into full battle mode.

She laughed recklessly. "Nothing much, but there are more coming. Mike's right, we can't leave that way. There's another exit downstairs, though we'll have to fight for it—come on!"

thirty-one

"Exterminate?" Evolet wrinkled his brow, listening to the order come through on Scarlet's walkie-talkie as they slipped out the back door of the laboratory and started across the long stretch of grounds between them and the Containment Facility.

The redhead shrugged. "Sounds like we might wanna hurry. But I'm going to shut this off," she went on, suiting action to the word as she spoke hurriedly, "and that way we can sneak in. Yes?"

"Yes," Evolet returned, still somewhat shocked at finding an ally here—and one like Scarlet. She sounded so matter-of-fact about everything—and then candidly revealed that she was only half-sure about it. Running a hand through his hair as usual, Evolet marched on, unconsciously increasing his speed.

Scarlet grinned and did the same thing, still holding tightly to her leather folder. "And we sneak in by the laser gate, no? Except Major Arcilla locked it permanently, so—"

"Then how do his soldiers intend to get into the building?" Evolet questioned, making a heroic act of self-control and tearing his hand out of his hair, shoving it into his pocket almost angrily.

Scarlet snapped her fingers. "Oh, good point! So he's going to unlock it."

"I would assume so," Evolet muttered dryly under his breath.

He was too used to thinking that anyone unfamiliar wasn't superhuman, so it was somewhat disconcerting when Scarlet grinned, having heard what he'd said. "And then we sneak in with them?"

"I don't know, do we?" Evolet shrugged violently. He stopped suddenly and turned to look at her. "Miss Dawes, you should probably head somewhere and stay safe. This doesn't involve you," he pointed out softly.

She shook her head defiantly. "Oh, but I'm a virus now! So, yes, it *does* involve me, no?"

"No," muttered Evolet, but this time she didn't hear him. Or maybe that was selective hearing.

"This war is in my DNA now. Besides, you might need this," she insisted firmly, gesturing with the folder.

"Okay, well, I'm about to do something to get over there in time," Evolet told her, whipping his hands out of his pockets suddenly. He motioned briefly over to where the security guards were crowding in through the laser gate. "So if you can follow, good and well. Otherwise—" He broke off, biting his lip.

"Fire away," Scarlet returned confidently. "I'll keep up."

"Whatever," Evolet shrugged, setting in motion the "something."

He broke into a fantastic run, his feet barely touching the ground as he fairly flew along. About five seconds later he'd reached the gate, so quickly that none of the laboratory security were expecting him—nor Scarlet, who was right behind.

Evolet shoved some aside and sent the others flying while the laser gate was still open, and before any of them had time to stop him or Scarlet the two were dodging darts and bullets and ducking into the building.

As Evolet tackled the five or six guards who'd already gotten inside, Scarlet slammed the door on the rest and proceeded to slide her ID card through the lock.

They could both hear the bolts sliding into the door, and when Evolet had finished knocking the last guard into unconsciousness, he glanced up.

Scarlet was already watching him. "That'll buy us some time," she told him, snapping her ID back onto her lapel and repositioning the leather folder under her arm. "Where to?"

"Where are the others?" Evolet asked in return.

Scarlet's red hair bobbed energetically as she jerked her head towards the elevators at the other end of the room. "Upstairs."

"Upstairs it is, then," Evolet decided, dashing off towards the heavy metal doors. Half a minute later, he and Scarlet were on their way up to the fourth floor.

"How long have you been superhuman?" he wondered aloud, having noticed by now that she seemed to be rather accustomed to it.

"About a week, today," Scarlet answered. She returned his glance easily. "You were born with it, right?"

"Right," Evolet nodded.

"What's that like?" Scarlet grinned.

"What's what—oh. Okay, I guess. I mean, yeah, I'm used to it," Evolet stuttered.

There was no time for further conversation, as the elevator pinged and the doors began to slide open. Evolet was out first, then Scarlet. They stopped and stared as they realized the hallway was empty and its doors were broken down.

"What!" Scarlet was shocked. "They're...already gone!"

Evolet was already racing down the hall. It took him less than a minute to see that every one of the rooms was empty. He looked at Scarlet. "Is that all of them?"

"Should be," Scarlet muttered. She began pointing and counting. "One, two, three... Yes, that's all. But where are they now?"

Evolet looked hard at her, and for a moment, the thought crossed his mind that this whole thing could be a ruse. But her blue eyes were so full of frank sincerity that he dismissed the suspicion.

"I don't know," he admitted. "Any ideas?"

Scarlet shook her head grimly. "No. None at all. They couldn't have gotten out...could they?"

"How many exits are there from this building?" Evolet asked quickly.

Scarlet ticked the exits off on her fingers. "There's the one we entered through... Then a fire escape off the roof...but that doesn't get past the laser fence unless we jump off the roof and maybe break our necks... Oh, there are some windows on the first floor...but that won't get us past the laser fence either...then... Oh, yes!"

She snapped her fingers, and a satisfied grin came over her face as she continued snapping them. "The laboratory underground—the one Doctor Schwann is finishing her cure in—it has tunnels that lead to the main building. But how would your friends have gotten into the laboratory? That's...that's top security—"

Evolet shrugged. "I don't know, but top security doesn't always look so secure when my siblings get their hands on it—"

"Not you?" Scarlet's eyebrows shot up.

He shrugged. "Well, the same for me, of course—but anyway, I'll bet that's where they've gone—but you said Doctor Schwann is finishing her cure in there?"

"Yes, she is, or that's what I heard, at least. Do you want me to show you how to get there?"

Evolet winced as they both heard a sudden gunshot, from far away in the building, but audible to their super-keen ears nonetheless. "Sounds good to me. What's the quickest way?"

thirty-two

Evolet and Scarlet had arrived too late.

Only a few minutes before the two got to the top floor, Jasmine and the others reached the downstairs laboratory—and were surprised to find Glenn's troop of soldiers waiting for them. Jasmine was the most surprised and annoyed of all, as she'd left the place smashed up and Eternyti locked in a closet.

But the soldiers didn't have a chance against a crowd of roused superhumans, and before they knew it they were either unconscious or running for their lives.

Jasmine noted annoyedly that Eternyti had taken advantage of her T4 to escape and take the Schwann3 machine with her.

"Maybe contaminating her wasn't such a good idea," she muttered, "but it's her fault. Everyone ready to go?" she added, glancing around. The others were mostly unscathed.

"You said there's a way out down here, right?" Petyr questioned, looking around doubtfully.

"There is," Jasmine assured him, stepping purposefully over to the part of the wall she'd seen Eternyti look at. She touched the outline of the secret door. Nothing happened, and Jasmine frowned.

She proceeded to push and pull at it. Still nothing.

"Let me try," came her twin sister's voice, and Alison shoved her aside distractedly, tugging at the door. When that didn't work, she kicked it.

"I can do that," Jasmine muttered, and gave the door a hearty, emphatic kick. It shook, but didn't budge. Jasmine's eyebrows shot up, and she growled in annoyance. Alison laughed mockingly.

"Hey, let's try this," Jason intervened before things got violent, stepping forward. He put his hand on the door, about eye level, as they'd seen the scientists and other faculty doing with other doors.

He was rewarded when a previously unnoticed light in the ceiling flickered on, shining on the door. The Eternity Labs logo shone faintly, along with the words *DNA Confirmation Required*.

"Hang it," Jasmine mumbled as everyone around, including her, gave a simultaneous sigh. Then she snapped her fingers. "*Yes!*"

Grabbing the purple-bladed knife from where she'd tucked it into her belt, Jasmine drove it into the border of the door tentatively. There was a slight bit of hesitation, but then the crystal bit through. Jasmine pulled it out with a triumphant laugh.

"Yes!" she shouted again, exultantly this time as she drove the blade home once more and continued slicing.

Next to her, Alison bounced impatiently from foot to foot. "Hurry!" she urged. "They're coming!"

"I know," Jasmine nodded distractedly. She, too, could hear the sounds of pursuit from a couple of floors above. Pounding feet, shouting, and radio static.

Meanwhile, Jason injected the six kids with paradraline. He was delighted and gratified to see that they seemed to recover themselves, even if they suddenly got sleepy. But there were enough people to carry them, and more. Petyr, Flynn, Tina, Jason, Alison, and Charles all shouldered one. Michael could handle himself.

Working swiftly but surely, Jasmine hacked through the door in a record-breaking time of forty-five seconds, eventually getting to the point where she judged it was good enough. She replaced the knife in her belt, stepped back a few feet, and ran forward, slamming her body into the door. The metal crumpled, and she leaped through the opening, grinning.

"Come on, let's go!" she shouted to her companions breathlessly. Nobody seemed to want to move first, so she stepped back out of the dark hallway and grabbed Michael's sleeve, pushing him through. Then Charles's.

"Come on, come on, hurry!" she urged as the other adults with the kids exited quickly.

Alison was the last, and she glanced back at her twin. "Come on yourself, Jaz!"

"I'm going to clean up after us," Jasmine retorted, still grinning, as she heard the noises of soldiers in the hallway outside the laboratory.

Alison heard them too. "Let's go, Jasmine," she told her slightly younger sister firmly.

Jasmine laughed, shaking her head. She gestured to the tired, frightened child perched atop Alison's shoulders. "Get that kid out of here, will you? I'll be along soon enough."

"Jaz—" Alison began, frowning.

"I'm not going to be stupid, Ali," Jasmine broke in impatiently. "I just need to clean the place up and set up something to cover our retreat. I'll be right along, okay?"

Alison bit her lip, but just then the little girl on her shoulders burst into tears. That seemed to decide the matter.

"Hurry up," she snapped, turning and dodging into the nearly black tunnel space.

Smiling lightly to herself, Jasmine swung around, then flew over to the main entry door at the other side of the room.

Using an ID card that she'd borrowed from one of the soldiers, she made the door close and lock, just as the elevator doors began to open.

Shots flew as the door closed the last few inches; Jasmine stepped out of the range of fire coolly, then hastened to initiate a complete lockdown. She knew she didn't have much time; Eternyti and Major Lucius Arcilla were on the other side of the door.

"Breathe, breathe, breathe," she muttered to herself, darting back and forth between the cabinets in the room.

She collected a small tin of kerosene and dumped it out on the floor of the tunnel entrance, making sure to splash the walls. That done, she cut a length of twine, soaked one end in kerosene, and dropped it in the doorway, then placed the other end in the laboratory.

Her fingers shook nervously as she pulled a lighter out of her pocket and set fire to the end of the twine. She waited.

The flame seemed to waver for a moment, then grew strong as it crept hungrily along the twine. Jasmine dropped the lighter back into her pocket.

"Fifteen to twenty seconds," she estimated to herself as she leaped hurriedly across the room and then over the kerosene spill.

The others were already out of sight—there was a sharp turn about ten feet into the tunnel. Jasmine waited there, breathlessly listening with her ear to the wall.

The seconds ticked by. She could hear her heart racing. Jasmine had never attempted a "clean-up" like this before.

Before ten seconds were up, the door had been opened. She could tell because suddenly the yelling got a lot louder, and a few guns went off, one of the bullets even landing in the tunnel.

Jasmine bit her lip, waiting. When would the kerosene catch fire?

The shouts and gunshots were so loud, and Jasmine so nervous, that she had no clue that someone else was in the tunnel until they rounded the corner, gun at the ready.

It was one of the guards, and Jasmine dealt with him as soon as she recovered from the brief flash of surprise, knocking his gun out of his hand and throwing him against the hard brick wall. He slumped down—but only to make way for another.

Someone had put out the fuse.

She was going to have to light it again.

Scowling, Jasmine knocked a few more guards out cold, pushing her way through the ten feet to the doorway.

Dozens more soldiers were in the laboratory, but Jasmine relatively ignored them, shooting absently with one hand and with the other pulling out the lighter again. Her fingers fumbled with the matchlock, and then she winced and gasped in pain as the fire-lighting mechanism was shot out of her hand.

Stopping shooting momentarily, she looked up and straight into the eyes of a determined-looking Major, and the other soldiers fell back.

"How about you come out here and fight your own battles instead of running and hiding," he invited, smiling pleasantly.

The corners of Jasmine's mouth curved slightly upwards into a grim smile. "Catch me if you can!"

Before Lucius could register the movement, Jasmine had darted out, past the kerosene, and into the laboratory. She brushed by the crowd of startled soldiers, who jumped back in shock and then looked themselves over anxiously to make sure they were still all there as she passed.

Before anyone had time to collect themselves and stop her, Jasmine had grabbed a blowtorch from the laboratory supplies and was heading back to the tunnel entrance.

But then someone blocked her, just in time.

Lucius.

He stood in the middle of the doorway. As she approached, he lifted his gun, swiftly yet deliberately, and took aim.

Jasmine looked up, saw him, and jumped aside.

But he'd already shot.

Jasmine froze for a moment, the force from the impact making her sway slightly before she recovered her balance.

The satisfied look that crossed Lucius's face gave her such a cold shock that she had to look down at herself before she realized she was completely fine—her jacket had stopped the bullet.

Her legs felt momentarily weak, and she laughed almost crazily for a moment—laughter which died from her lips as Lucius shot again, at the blowtorch and at her hand.

For the third time in fifteen minutes Jasmine winced and clenched her hand tightly.

"Seriously!" she muttered, angrily tossing what remained of the blowtorch to the ground.

Brushing her hands together in intense pain, she looked up and forced a challenging grin at the soldiers who now crowded around her, emboldened by their leader's bit of success.

"First come first served!"

"Get her!" Lucius shouted. "Dead or alive!"

"Why don't you do your own dirty work yourself," Jasmine retorted, shoving a hapless soldier away from her.

Someone snuck up behind her with a gun, and she flipped it out of his hand without even turning around.

Jasmine shook her head, frowning. "Really, though, it would be nice if you'd just let me leave," she remarked, borrowing someone's dart gun and making the wall a target. "I'm kind of in a hurry and I don't want to hurt anybody—"

"That's what you all say," came a sudden hiss from behind her, and Jasmine wheeled to face an angry and dangerous-looking Eternyti.

The scientist's usually neat red hair was in a shambles, there was an uncovered but mostly healed cut on her arm from where Jasmine had rather unprofessionally injected her, and there was blood smeared on her latex gloves—and on the gun they held, aimed neatly at Jasmine's face.

Without blinking, Jasmine batted it away, pulling a face. "When will guns go obsolete?" she wondered aloud, wrenching it out of Eternyti's hand suddenly and smashing it against a wall.

Eternyti shouted in annoyance, ignoring the gun and jumping at Jasmine. She might not have been as trained or as used to being superhuman, but there was still that spark of savage instinct in her that can be found in everyone, from couch potatoes to Navy SEALs, and it definitely showed in Eternyti as she forced Jasmine to retreat.

But Jasmine was perfectly content to back up, especially when she managed to get in the middle of the doorway to the tunnel to block any more soldiers from coming through. Then she put up a fight in earnest, grabbing hold of a jagged piece of metal from the long-demolished door and holding it up as a temporary shield.

Eternyti charged her again and shoved her over. Jasmine landed hard in the puddle of kerosene, scowling as she jumped back up.

"Dude, *why!*" she muttered in protest, looking around for something to block the doorway. "Maybe I shouldn't have cut through the doo—"

She never finished the sentence. A dart finally found her, and after a moment of frozen shock, Jasmine toppled over.

* * *

She began to wake up a few minutes later, finding herself strapped to a section of the laboratory wall.

It took her a few seconds to realize where she was and what was going on; she opened her eyes, taking in the scene of a completely totaled laboratory and the last of the guards disappearing through the tunnel entrance.

Jasmine bit her lip and tried to jerk herself away from the wall. But it was futile. The straps that bound her were too strong. She had no idea what they were made of, but she couldn't break them.

Though Jasmine didn't know it, the straps were the same make of material that had been used by the Violet Army years before.

She shut her eyes, trying to ignore the slightly ebbing waves of pain from her shattered hand and cut shoulder. The bandage had come loose, but of course she couldn't reach it. At least it wasn't bleeding too much, but as it was, she was feeling somewhat weaker than usual.

Jasmine forced herself to breathe. The pain wouldn't last forever. It never did. That was part of being superhuman—even if she could stand injuries on a whole new scale from what the average human could bear, she healed much more quickly.

But her eyes flew open again in spite of herself a moment later when she heard a meaningful cough.

After a half-second or so of looking furtively around, she saw the Major, standing near the main door, watching Jasmine and fingering the small purple crystal dagger that was changing hands so many times that night.

Eternyti was in the room, too, Jasmine realized with a mix of relief and the closest thing to fear she'd ever gotten; the scientist was ignoring her, setting the Schwann3 machine in motion once again. Jasmine sighed.

Major Arcilla was still panting hard, unlike Jasmine or Eternyti, and his eyes gleamed hard and cold as he watched Jasmine.

A small smile of grim satisfaction came over his face when he saw that she couldn't escape the bonds, but still he didn't say anything. It was up to Jasmine to start a conversation. Something which she did not do, but instead closed her eyes again and let herself hang limply.

She was tired. Incredibly so.

"Two minutes, Major," came Eternyti's voice. Jasmine realized with a small burst of shock that Eternyti sounded tired, too. "Two minutes and it'll be ready."

"Good," Lucius replied softly, straightening away from the wall.

Jasmine's keen ears picked up his footsteps, and so, without opening her eyes, she could follow his progress across the room to a couple of feet in front of her.

Instinct was screaming for her to break out somehow and get away, but she knew she couldn't—at least not yet—so she feigned exhaustion even as she recovered swiftly, and ignored the Major.

But he wasn't going to ignore her.

"You don't have to pretend—twin," he began, smiling lightly. "Which one is it? Alison or Jasmine?"

Jasmine didn't deign to give him an answer, so he went on, still smiling in a way that would've made her blood run cold had she had her eyes open to see it.

"You know, I've been eager to meet you—or one of you Whytes, at least—for quite a while now. Do you know who I am?"

"String, or nothing," Jasmine muttered under her breath, squeezing her eyes shut tighter as she felt her pulse racing.

Lucius wasn't amused, and he passed over the remark without calling attention to it, though he dropped his smile. "Your father? Conner Whyte? You know him?"

"Are you kidding," Jasmine growled, unable to ignore that one.

"Yes? Good, then."

"You seem to say that a lot," the eighteen-year-old noted aloud, determined to make the best of the situation. Right now, she was keenly aware that Lucius was holding the only knife she knew of that could cut through her jacket—and, presumably, through the straps as well.

Again Lucius ignored her, and his eyes flashed. "Anyway, my father was a policeman. Dominic Arcilla. Have you ever heard of him?"

"Not that I'm aware of." Jasmine figured he was probably getting impatient for a real answer by now.

"Okay, well, he was in Annapolis when the Purple Blitzkrieg broke out, Miss Whyte." Lucius's face suddenly grew darker as, for the first time, Jasmine opened her eyes and looked at him. She felt she knew what was coming, and she soon discovered she was quite right.

"Your mother—Violet Arnnu—had him killed. And when my father tried to escape, she had that minion of hers do the job."

His face contorted. "*Your father.*"

"I'm sorry," Jasmine told him quite simply and genuinely, but Lucius couldn't care less for her sympathy. It was too late for that, and now he wanted something else.

"Listen well, Miss Whyte, because what you say next can very well affect the way you leave this room."

Jasmine waited expectantly as he paused a moment to take a deliberate breath.

"I hear from my scouts that your aunt has left Annapolis, with both your parents. They've gone off the radar. I had someone search your aunt's place, but they've very obviously upped and gone, and they probably intend to leave the country. Where to, you would know better than I would.

"That's where my proposition comes in, Miss Whyte. You tell me where they're headed, and I'll let you leave here for wherever you like. My men and I will leave you alone. And you have five minutes now to tell me. If you don't, well—"

He grimaced. "It depends on whether you prefer Schwann3 or—"

After a sideways glance at Eternyti, who was moving the vial of Schwann3 to a smaller machine, Lucius slid his gloved index finger across his throat meaningfully.

Jasmine shook her head slowly. Her light blue eyes flitted to see Eternyti's progress—then she returned her attention to the Major.

"I'm sorry for your loss, and I'm sure Mom and Dad would be too," she told him, choosing her words carefully. "But as you probably already realize, I can't do that, and I'm not—"

Lucius held up a finger. "Stop right there, Miss Whyte. You don't want to finish saying that."

"But I do," Jasmine insisted, narrowing her eyes.

A smile came back on Lucius's face. "No, you don't understand. I need to talk to them," he went on seriously. "I need to *talk*—"

"And that's why you wait until they're weak and helpless, right?" Jasmine countered, her eyes flashing. "I know there are a lot of people that don't like my parents, but most don't seem to realize that Mom has reformed and Dad wasn't in his right mind—"

"We don't need to go into details, Miss Whyte," Lucius interrupted firmly. "Just tell me where they're headed and you can be out of here."

Her light blue eyes met his dark ones. "I told you no," Jasmine told him a few seconds later, just as firmly.

Lucius clicked his tongue softly, and suddenly he seemed to reach a decision. Jasmine breathed a sigh of relief as he stepped away from her, still holding the knife—a sigh that quickly turned into a sharply in-drawn gasp as he approached Eternyti. "Doctor Schwann, could I borrow one of your little antidotes?"

Eternyti nodded briefly, obviously preoccupied as she quickly selected one of the syringes and handed it to Lucius. The rest she gathered into a small container—except for one, which she held in her hand. Turning, she stared almost blankly at Jasmine—and the Major.

Neither of them were paying any attention to her. Lucius broke off the syringe cap; as he stepped closer to Jasmine, she clenched her teeth and fists and fought the bonds as best as she could. But it was useless.

"I really would stop moving if I were you," Lucius cautioned almost anxiously, hovering the needle above her left—and uninjured—wrist. "Don't want to accidentally inject yourself, do you?"

He didn't wait for an answer, and as Jasmine saw the sense in his advice and grudgingly stopped struggling, he looked directly at her.

"I'm only asking you this one more time, Miss Whyte. Where do your parents intend to take refuge?"

Jasmine winced as the tip of the needle bit through her skin. Lucius held his thumb quite readily over the pusher, waiting.

"Well?" he asked softly, finally.

"I told you—I'm not telling you!" Jasmine gritted out, raising her voice in frustration. She squeezed her eyes shut tight, waiting for the further prick she knew was going to come.

thirty-five

"Where?" Evolet demanded of Scarlet for probably the fifth time in the past five minutes. He was getting rather impatient, especially when the gunshots they were hearing suddenly stopped.

Scarlet had been in doubt for a moment, but then she tore off down a hallway. "It's this way, I told you," she returned quickly, still holding her folder tightly with one hand and then her ID card in the other. She slid it in the doorway; but instead of flashing green like it usually did, it flashed red instead.

Her shoulders slumped in defeat.

"They've locked it—and all the other doors—and I don't have the authority to get past it," she explained dejectedly. "And we were so close. Only two more hallways."

"Out of the way," Evolet commanded brusquely, retreating to the far end of the hallway and stopping there a moment, waiting for Scarlet to get away from the door.

"Huh?" she asked, blinking.

"I said out of the way!" Evolet shouted, and as he began running towards the door, it finally dawned on Scarlet what he intended to do. Jumping out of the way just in time, she watched in awe as he slammed into the door. It shook on its hinges, and Evolet fell back, panting and rubbing his arms ruefully, hopping on one leg.

"Okay, maybe not such a good idea," he wheezed.

Scarlet eyed him anxiously. "What if we try that again—together?"

Two minutes later found them both charging the second door. Then the next. And then—they were in the laboratory.

Evolet took in the scene immediately: Eternyti loading liquid-filled syringes into a portable container, and Jasmine strapped against a wall, with the Major about to inject her with Schwann3.

Evolet caught his breath, and then did the only thing he could think of at the moment—yelled as loudly as he could.

"Fire!"

Jasmine's eyes flew open, and the Major turned his head slightly, just enough to see that it was Evolet, though he couldn't see Scarlet where she was behind him. He didn't move the syringe.

"Don't come a step nearer, Evolet Whyte, or your sister here—" Lucius clicked his tongue meaningfully.

"Get your poison away from her, Major," Evolet gritted through clenched teeth. But he didn't come any closer.

Lucius shook his head, smiling slightly. "That's not how the game goes, Evolet. I said stay away."

Evolet winced as he saw Jasmine tense suddenly and he realized Lucius was actually ready and prepared to inject her. "If you don't get that needle away from her, you're not leaving this room alive," he threatened, trying to keep his voice level. "She can't hurt you. Deal with *me*, Lucius!"

But the Major ignored the challenge, or so it seemed. "Doctor Schwann, could you come here a moment, please?"

Looking startled, Eternyti obliged, taking the syringe from him. Smiling grimly, Lucius turned to face Evolet.

"Rather stupid of you to come alone. And you know what? I'm going to take you up on that." A strange light came into the Major's eyes. "Why do you look so much like your mother?"

"Wh—a—t?" Evolet was completely taken aback, as much by the seemingly random comment about his mother as by the remark that he was alone. Confused, he took a moment to look behind him, and realized suddenly that Scarlet had disappeared.

The Major laughed, noting his surprise. "What, did you think she'd be here? Violet Whyte, née Arnnu, risking her life for some irrelevant—"

"Take that back," Evolet flared suddenly, clenching his fists.

Lucius shook his head derisively and went on nonetheless.

"—But then again, she's too busy fleeing."

Suddenly his face got serious. "Where are your parents headed?"

"That's none of your business," Evolet returned easily, watching some subtle movement behind the Major. His eyes brightened.

Lucius either didn't notice, or didn't take heed of the fact. "Well then, it's too bad for your sister, because—"

He stopped suddenly. It would be hard for anyone to finish a sentence when hit over the head suddenly with a chair, especially when that chair was wielded with superhuman strength. Utterly surprised and quite literally shocked, Lucius crumpled to the floor, temporarily unconscious.

Evolet grinned at Scarlet as she replaced the chair carefully on the ground and flipped across the room to where Eternyti was staring at her in surprise. The younger scientist took advantage of that surprise to promptly brush Eternyti's hand—and the syringe—away from Jasmine's wrist and grin at the slightly younger girl who had no clue what was going on.

"Evy?" Jasmine called out hesitantly. "Who's this?"

Meanwhile Evolet carefully relieved the fallen Major of his knife, and then headed over to the two, casting a sideways glance at Eternyti as he did so. She was back at the counter, leaning against it, watching them aimlessly. Evolet got the impression she wasn't going to do anything.

"Her name is Scarlet Wh—Dawes," Evolet corrected himself hastily, flushing red as he used the knife to slice through his younger sister's bonds. "You okay?" he asked her anxiously.

"Scarlet Dawes?" Jasmine echoed, stretching gingerly and keeping a suspicious eye on the older scientist. "She's a redhead. I don't trust red hair anymore."

"We'll talk about it later, Jaz! We have to hurry!" Evolet tossed the knife away and touched the bandage on his sister's shoulder.

He frowned. It was a *mess*.

Someone gasped behind him, and Evolet spun around.

"Scarlet Dawes?" Eternyti stared incredulously at the young woman. "*You?*"

"Yeah, me," Scarlet replied, dropping her smile as she gestured at the container of syringes. "Those don't work, Doctor Schwann. I'm not kidding you. I—"

"You gave yourself T6." Eternyti's tone was cold in disbelief.

"I found a cure," Scarlet told her quickly. "A real cure."

Eternyti shook her head. "But if you're still superhuman, then it's not a cure—"

"Superhuman isn't a disease," Scarlet shrugged easily, frowning as she clutched her leather folder tighter.

Meanwhile, Evolet was busily rebandaging Jasmine's shoulder. "He didn't hurt you, did he?" he asked her anxiously.

"Not really. We Whytes are hard to kill," Jasmine reminded him, glancing at her thrice-wounded hand and sighing woefully. But then she got businesslike, as usual. "Evy, we need to go and make sure the others are getting away safely. I think the whole troop went through the tunnels after them. Oh, and—"

"Yeah?" he returned, pulling off one of his gloves and handing it to her. "Put that on your hand, if you can—it won't soak in. What were you trying to say?"

Jasmine winced as she gingerly pulled the glove onto her hand. "Evy, he's going after Mom and Dad. We have to warn them."

"Yeah, we can do that—eventually," Evolet grinned. "Hand okay?"

"I guess," she shrugged, but then Evolet pulled off his jacket as well and started wrapping it around her arm.

"That might help. Come on, let's go!" he urged, noticing that Lucius was beginning to wake up.

Scarlet had been keeping an eye on Eternyti, but now she walked off briskly in the direction of the tunnel, after a parting remark to the older scientist. "Believe me, Doctor Schwann—you don't need a cure!"

She stopped short on seeing the liquid on the ground. "What's this?"

"Kerosene," Jasmine retorted, coming up behind her. "Evy, got a lighter?"

"Better, a match," her brother responded, pushing her gently through the doorway and stepping in himself. He glanced at Jasmine and Scarlet, then back through the doorway at Eternyti and Lucius.

Pulling a matchbook out of his pocket with his gloveless hand, Evolet struck one, held it out over the kerosene, and then, with a final glance at Lucius, who was stumbling to his feet, dropped the match.

"Matches are better than lighters?" Jasmine muttered dubiously, but Evolet ignored the comment.

The kerosene ignited immediately, and the flames shot up even as high as Evolet's face as he jumped back away from the sudden heat and turned to follow his sister and newfound acquaintance out through the tunnel. They walked at first, but then they began running.

Behind them in the laboratory, Lucius stood up when the flames were at their strongest. He watched the three disappear, his eyes burning as vengefully and heatedly as the flames themselves.

"You won't get away. We'll be meeting again. I promise! You cannot hide forever, you Whytes!"

Shaking off his apathy, he ran to the laboratory counter against which Eternyti was still leaning, and picked up the case of syringes. Without another word, he dashed off through the normal laboratory entrance, leaving Eternyti behind.

She stared at the vial still in her hand, and then closed her fingers around it, an almost fanatic look coming into her blue-green eyes.

Before she could change her mind, she pulled off the cap—nearly breaking the needle as she did—and stabbed it into her arm.

She fell back against the counter, gasping for breath. The Schwann3 burned like fire, and she realized dimly that she was screaming.

This hadn't happened to Violet or Conner or Joyce though—why not?

Through a myriad of confused thoughts, the answer came to her: they had been unconscious.

And she was not.

She wished she was, having already realized that this was no cure. She was on the ground now, helpless, unable to move, hardly able to breathe.

It was going to kill her.

What had she done? This was so horrible she found herself amazed that the three test subjects had survived. She should have done more research, experimented further. This was *not* a cure!

And suddenly she realized, Lucius had the other doses.

He was going to try to give it to the Whytes, the Foleys, Scarlet Dawes, and—

Tnhe children.

Eternyti's blood ran cold at the thought.

No.

She tried to get up, but the effort was too much, and she fell down again, her eyes closing over. She fought the dizzy feeling, telling herself she had to stop the Major. Somehow she reached a walkie-talkie someone had dropped. Eternyti pulled it over to herself, using all her remaining energy to hold the button down while she talked.

"Major. It's not the cure. Major?"

Eternyti didn't get an answer. She wanted to scream.

"Major Arcilla, it's not the cure! You can't give it to them! Listen to me!"

thirty-six

At the fence, everything was going well, and under Jason's direction soon all of the younger children were over the fence, along with their carriers. Jason pointed his older brother Petyr in the direction of where they'd left their evacuation vans, and soon his five companions were on their way.

Still carrying his passenger, Jason glanced back; Michael was still on the other side of the fence, about halfway up, climbing slowly.

"Come on, Mike!" Jason shouted encouragingly, grinning up at him, though the boy couldn't see his face in the darkness. "We gotta hurry!"

"Coming," came the faint reply.

Jason could see lights in the distance now—lights, and figures. He saw them after he began to hear the shouting, and he tensed. "You're running out of time!"

The kid on his back mumbled something sleepily as Jason stared up at Michael and the boy on the fence suddenly stopped. Michael waited there a moment without moving, and then, much to Jason's surprise and astonishment, he started climbing back down—on the wrong side.

Jason's eyes opened wide in disbelief. "Michael!"

"I'm going to stop them!" Michael shouted back, jumping easily to the ground and turning briefly to glance at Jason.

Jason had his flashlight on now, and the beams glinted off Michael's eyes—now completely coral. Jason bit his lip.

"No, Michael, just come on over!" he yelled desperately, with a sinking feeling that he probably shouldn't try to tackle Michael with another kid on his back.

Michael just gestured towards the soldiers. "I'll be right back! I can stop them!" he assured Jason, heading off slowly at first but then faster.

Jason got the awful feeling he was dealing with someone on drugs. "MICHAEL LEBLANC!" he screamed out in a last desperate attempt to bring Michael back to himself.

It failed. Michael ignored him completely.

Jason was just about to leave the kid on the ground and go after Michael, when he saw a commotion among the soldiers, and three figures broke clear of the rest, heading in a dead, superhuman run for the fence. Evolet, Jasmine, and—someone else. Jason breathed a sigh of relief; now everyone was accounted for.

"Evy!" he yelled at the top of his lungs. "Stop Michael! I'll be ready when you guys get over!"

That said, he saw Evolet saluting in recognition of the command, and the twenty-year-old headed off to block the younger boy. Satisfied, Jason sped off after the others.

Evolet caught up to Michael and stopped him with a magnificent dive that would've gotten him on any football team. He was startled when the boy attacked him furiously, punching and kicking for all he was worth.

Scarlet and Jasmine came up with them then, Scarlet staring and Jasmine glancing behind them at the quickly oncoming soldiers and muttering something under her breath.

"Paradraline," she told Evolet quickly, glancing down at her belt and then biting her lip. "I haven't got any left—"

"I do," Evolet reminded her, retrieving one of his own and administering the dose to Michael with the same attention as if it'd been an epi-pen.

Michael retaliated by screaming and kicking Evolet solidly in the stomach. The young man fell back, gasping for breath for a moment or so, though he was more confused than winded.

"It's not working," Jasmine realized, sticking out a foot and tripping Michael as he tried to run past her. "Why not?"

Evolet grabbed Michael's ankle and jerked him down on the ground roughly, with just a touch of his own annoyance coming through in the action. "I don't know!"

"Try this," Scarlet spoke up suddenly behind him, definitely worried about the soldiers who were catching up quickly. "We've only got seconds and this is an emergency. He'd kill himself."

Evolet wheeled around, still sitting on the ground, to see the young redhead scientist handing him a small, blue-liquid-filled syringe. He took it, and stared at it a moment, and then back at Michael, just as the boy shouted in between screams of pure wild fury that he was going to kill them all, *now*.

"What is that?" Jasmine breathed, looking at Scarlet suspiciously.

"Stabilizer." Scarlet was watching Evolet intently as his hand with the syringe hovered over Michael's wrist doubtfully. "It works. I'm alive and well."

Evolet shut his eyes tightly. "Jaz, should I?"

"Well, duh, if it works!" Jasmine yelled at him. "Come on, we have to go!"

With his eyes still squeezed shut, Evolet injected Michael once again. Michael didn't even seem to notice the sting, but he stopped struggling, and when Evolet glanced cautiously at his eyes, the coral color was leaving them. Evolet breathed a sigh of relief.

"Come on, come on, we have to get over the fence now," Scarlet interjected impatiently. "He's going to be weaker in a few minutes—and we are OUT OF TIME!"

She shouted the last three words, having turned around to pitch into a soldier who'd caught up with them. The soldier crumpled to the ground, and suddenly Scarlet found herself shoved behind Jasmine, who was facing the same direction now.

"You haven't got a jacket like mine," Jasmine reminded her breathlessly. "Get Michael over the fence!"

Seconds later the four had dealt with the closest pursuers and had reached the high electric fence. Evolet got Michael climbing immediately, especially as Scarlet warned him it was any minute now before Michael would suddenly find himself getting weaker. Scarlet glanced at her hands and frowned, but then Evolet tossed her a pair of leather gloves.

"Oh, thanks," she murmured, slipping them on.

Jasmine glanced at her brother warily, aware that he only had one pair of spares and he'd donated the first pair for her injured hand. "What about you, Evolet Whyte?" she asked dryly.

"I'll be fine," Evolet breezed, testing the fence with his bare hand and wincing momentarily. "It's—only as strong as last time."

"I could climb and then toss them over," Scarlet volunteered, feeling very much in the way.

Evolet shook his head. "Nah, we don't have time. Let's go!"

thirty-seven

It was around then that Major Lucius Arcilla finally emerged from the Containment Facility, holding the case of Schwann3 tightly as he made his way to a control room located across the laboratory compound. As he hurried along, he couldn't help but see that the superhumans were making their getaway. He bit his cut lip.

"Glenn, I'm going to be doubling the electric fence strength," he spoke quickly into his walkie-talkie. "Stop them from getting away. All I need....is one Whyte—alive."

"Okay, Major," Glenn replied faintly—and then crackled off. Lucius shrugged, racing on towards the building to increase the fence power before the superhumans could cross it. But even as he ran, something came through from Eternyti—an urgent warning not to use the Schwann3. Lucius ignored it, smiling grimly as he flipped his walkie-talkie off and entered the small room, hitting the light switch quickly.

It took him only about a second to find the panel that controlled the fence, and then a second more to glance at the display.

7,000 volts, he read.

He punched in a new level. *15,000.*

Warning: This Level of Electricity May Prove Fatal. Are You Sure You Want to Continue?

Yes, Lucius told the machine, watching satisfiedly as the screen flashed the word *Charging*. Then it flashed green, and the new number came on the screen.

Success!

***

"You okay, Jaz?" Evolet was asking his sister anxiously for what was probably the twentieth time, as they neared the top of the fence.

Jasmine scowled, trying to concentrate on what she was doing. "Evolet Whyte, if you ask me that again I'll knock you down," she gritted.

"Okay, okay," Evolet murmured apologetically, flinching slightly as he found a new handhold. It was a rather tedious process, grabbing hold of new wires and dealing with a new feeling of shock each time.

Scarlet, who was about even with the other two, laughed softly. "I think he's just worried about you, Miss Whyte."

"It's Jaz," Jasmine muttered almost begrudgingly.

"Jaz." Scarlet tested out the new word and laughed again, almost recklessly.

"Mike, you okay down there?" Evolet shouted, reaching the top of the fence and flipping over it, grabbing ahold of the other side and beginning to lower himself down. Scarlet and Jasmine began to do the same a few seconds later.

"Yeah," came a faint reply from the figure huddled on the ground. Michael had just barely gotten down when he was struck by the wave of dizziness, which, Scarlet assured them, would soon wear off. So he was resting now.

Evolet was about to answer him, when suddenly something sparked on the wires nearer to the fencepost. He paused, watching it dubiously—and then his mouth opened in a silent scream and his hair stood on end, literally, as 15,000 volts of electricity shot through him, also literally.

"Ev—" Jasmine felt the sudden heat through her gloves and boots, and tensed, glancing at her brother. Her eyebrows shot up. He was quite literally glued to the fence, completely electrified.

"Blast," she muttered, glancing at Scarlet, who was looking at the fence with something of panic coming over her face.

"Uhh, Jaz, what do we do?" the scientist stammered nervously, glancing down thirty feet to the ground.

"Knock him off," Jasmine directed her suddenly, jerking her head towards Evolet. "Idiot got no gloves."

"Wh—a—t?" Scarlet questioned, staring at her incredulously.

"Knock him off the fence!" Jasmine repeated impatiently, carefully maneuvering herself downward a foot or so.

Scarlet gaped a moment or two longer, then finally registered the command and hesitantly tried to brush Evolet's bare hands off the fence. It didn't work—he'd been holding on tightly before being electrocuted.

"Harder!" Jasmine urged, looking up briefly before continuing down. "We can't just leave him there!"

Bracing herself, Scarlet managed to shove Evolet hard enough that he came loose. Without even a scream, he tumbled down to the ground, about twenty-three feet. Scarlet winced, but Jasmine was already halfway down, and she didn't know how much longer her gloves were going to hold out.

Quickly she scrambled down, arriving at about the same time as Jasmine. The Whyte girl glanced at her briefly.

"How's your patient?" she wondered aloud, and Scarlet went to inspect Michael, while Jasmine took a look at her older brother.

Scarlet found Michael to be sitting up, recovering. He smiled weakly at her, with a look of genuine surprise and disbelief in his now completely-green eyes. "It's gone," he breathed. "Completely gone."

"Gone?" Scarlet repeated, beaming. "Good!"

"It's a nice birthday present," he murmured, closing his eyes and then opening them again happily and looking around him as if he was seeing his surroundings for the first time.

He stared at the young scientist and realized—he didn't know her. "Who are you?" the now thirteen-year-old demanded frankly.

"A friend," Scarlet returned, grinning. "Scarlet Dawes. And you are—?"

"Michael Leblanc," Michael told her. "But you can call me Mike. Do you have a nickname?"

"That would be weird," Jasmine interjected from a short distance away, muttering.

Scarlet shook her head. "Not really."

"Okay, then—and here comes Uncle Jason. Let's go, everyone!" Jasmine added energetically as they all heard the first sounds of a motorcycle.

Scarlet glanced around at them: Jasmine, Michael, Evolet, and herself. She frowned. "All of us on a motorcycle?"

"Not a normal motorcycle," Jasmine smirked. "We'll fit!"

thirty-eight

No one had ever seen Lucius madder than he was when he got the report that every single one of the superhumans had made it clean away. Even Glenn couldn't understand his intensity, especially when he told her and his other higher-ranking officers that they had to find out where the Whytes had gone and how. Then he picked up a small plastic container of syringes and showed it to them.

"This is Schwann3—you know, what Doctor Schwann was perfecting when they attacked the laboratory. It's also going to be our weapon when we find out where they've gone. This time, we have to stop them *forever*."

His face was hard-set and determined.

"We're only going to have one more chance. This insanity is spreading again."

* * *

In the secondary getaway van, in which Jason, Jasmine, Scarlet, Michael, Evolet, and a few of the kids were beginning their trip across Texas to Mexico, spirits were dampened, though not completely out. The night was dark, the road—or non-road—was bumpy, and to top it all off, Evolet was still unconscious and Jasmine was wondering if she trusted Scarlet to try to fix up her hand, as Jason was driving.

"Spreading" had never been further from their minds. Michael was falling asleep with the other kids in the back seat, Evolet was sprawled on the next seat up, and Jasmine and Scarlet had taken the seat behind Jason in the driver's. Scarlet was still holding her folder of T6S. She glanced sideways at Jasmine as the eighteen-year-old struggled to disengage her hand from Evolet's glove and then her own highly damaged one.

Finally Scarlet spoke up. "I took a couple years of medical school… Do you want me to help?"

"Yes, please," Jasmine admitted, giving up immediately and holding out her hand for Scarlet's inspection.

Gingerly, Scarlet peeled the two layers of glove off. The first thing she said was a genuine, frank, unrestrained "Oww."

"What?" Jasmine murmured, having shut her eyes tightly.

"I—I dunno," the redhead muttered, closing her own eyes and taking a deep breath before she opened them again. "I—uh—"

"Whatever." Jasmine forced herself to open her eyes, and blinked as she stared.

"Okay. Yeah, oww is right. It doesn't hurt as much, but I hope that doesn't mean it's healing like that…"

"Can you move anything?" Scarlet demanded, trying to sound and look professional as she took in the mess of bone and blood and torn skin, reaching hastily for a paper towel before it dripped on the Whyte girl's clothes.

"Uhh—no," Jasmine returned decidedly, flinching at the attempt. "What are you gonna do?"

"Not much till we get you to a hospital or something," Scarlet decided, regaining some of her confidence. "We *can* do that, right? Do you have a first aid kit anywhere?" she added, looking around the van helplessly.

"Naturally," Jason spoke up from the front seat, glancing behind momentarily before hurriedly turning his attention back to the road again. "Actually, sorry, I don't know—"

"We do," Jasmine broke in, jerking her right hand away from Scarlet so she could bend down and grab the required item from underneath the seat. The redhead clicked her tongue in annoyance.

"Stay still!" she ordered, beginning the process of delicately trying to clean Jasmine's hand as best as she could. Jasmine winced and pulled faces in turn.

"There's a hospital half an hour away," Jason noted, juggling his phone in one hand and driving crazily with the other. Luckily for them, they were driving on a dirt road at night, and no one else was on it. "I'll head that way and we can get you patched up, Jaz. How's Evy?"

"Still out cold," Jasmine reported, glancing around despite an urgent protest from Scarlet for her to not move. "I think he's alive."

"You think?" The tone of Jason's voice rose in concern. "Well, is he breathing?"

Scarlet checked this time. "Yes," she mumbled absently, turning her attention back to Jasmine's hand. "I expect he's just shocked—oh, sorry."

"Should we wake him up?" Jason muttered dubiously.

"Hurry up with my hand, I'll do it," Jasmine volunteered, glancing at the redhead impatiently.

"Stop moving or I won't be able to do anything," Scarlet retorted, trying to finish wrapping Jasmine's hand tightly in gauze before the eighteen-year-old moved around suddenly again. A few seconds later she twisted it and tore it off. "There you go. Best I can do."

"Thanks," Jasmine murmured dubiously, turning around. She hadn't bothered to buckle, and now she leaned halfway over the seat, reaching out with her good, left hand. "Ev!"

"You're blocking my view of the road," Jason yelled annoyedly.

"Well, sorry," Jasmine muttered, hesitating.

"Just hurry it up," Jason shrugged, glancing at his phone again and then speeding up the van.

Ignoring the jerk, Jasmine batted at her older brother's face with her good hand. "Hey. Evy! Wake up!"

After a few repeated attempts to awaken her brother that way, Jasmine decided to change tactics, and grabbed a water bottle from the front of the van instead, opening it with her teeth and then carefully dumping an ounce or so in her brother's face. He sat up suddenly, spluttering and gasping, and nearly rolled off the seat. Jasmine casually recapped the bottle, grinning at her brother in the rear-view mirror.

"Awake now?" she asked him, still smirking. Covering her mouth with her hand, Scarlet flipped around in her seat to watch the fireworks.

The eldest of the Whyte children sat up, rubbing his head. "Owwww," he moaned, and then stared at the two like he didn't know them.

His eyes faltered for a moment and then came into focus.

"Who am I?"

Jasmine pulled a face. "Evolet Whyte! Don't play stupid."

"Evolet Whyte? What kind of name is that?" Evolet spluttered, his hand going to his hair subconsciously and running through it with a savage gesture of annoyance. "Who am I? Where am I? Who are you?"

Jasmine looked exasperated as it became obvious her older brother really was the victim of amnesia. "Memory loss? That's a first. How do we fix that, Doctor?" she asked, turning to Scarlet.

The young red-haired scientist lifted her hands in a gesture of complete ignorance. "How would I know? But in books they do it by cracking the person over the head with something," she added reflectively, clapping her mouth shut as she realized Jasmine was the type to actually do that sort of thing, and powerfully, too.

"Good point." A dark smile came over Jasmine's face.

"No—" Scarlet began, in a panic, but the Whyte girl was already addressing her brother again.

"Okay, my dear Evy, you have a choice—"

"Just tell me who I am," the stranger Evolet interrupted, his confused purple eyes flashing dangerously. "Why am I here?"

"—and I'm only going to say it once," Jasmine went on, unperturbed despite the fact that Evolet suddenly grabbed the back of her seat, looking violent. "Do you want me to hit you over the head, or do you prefer to do it yourself?"

"Do you take me for an idiot—" Spluttering, Evolet stood up suddenly, accidentally knocking himself good and hard on the roof of the van. The vehicle shook, and Evolet fell over, dazed into unconsciousness—again.

Jasmine couldn't repress a gleeful laugh as she reached for the water bottle again. "Here goes number two!"

"I would say don't get the car wet or it'll mold, but I don't think it's mine," Jason interjected cheerfully from the driver's seat.

Scarlet would've gaped at him, but she was too busy watching Jasmine wet her brother's face once more. This time when he came to himself, he did it roaring.

"Who's dumping water in my face—! Why are we in the car—oh—oh—OH!" This last exclamation was accompanied by Evolet's shaking his head vigorously as he took in his surroundings.

He glared at Jasmine, who was smirking. "Remember now?"

"Duh I remember," Evolet snapped. "Got fried against an electric fence. That's what I get for lending you my gloves—"

"You lent them to her, not to me," Jasmine interrupted, jerking her head in Scarlet's direction, who immediately turned her gaze back to the front of the van to hide the relieved flush creeping over her face.

"Oh, yeah." Evolet suddenly coughed, and then choked. "Fine, then."

Jasmine snorted. "You're so eager to blame me instead, eh? Hey, are you okay?" she demanded suddenly, looking hard at him. "You were right when you said 'fried.'"

"Yeah, I guess I'm alright, but my head hurts," Evolet muttered, blinking rapidly for a few seconds. "How long have I been out?"

"Fifteen, twenty minutes," Jason informed him. "We're on the way to the hospital for Jasmine's hand."

"What about my brain?" Evolet sniffed, then laughed at the annoyed look that came over Jasmine's face. "Just kidding. Say, where's Michael? Is he alright?" he demanded, climbing back up onto the seat.

Silence. Evolet looked behind him in a fright.

"Oh, he's asleep," he realized, chuckling. Then he glanced upfront again. "You know, Miss Dawes, I hope that concoction of yours doesn't have any long-term effects. I know it was an emergency, but—"

"I wouldn't know," she confessed, frowning. "I hope it's alright. I mean, I only just got it myself. But I feel fine," she pointed out. "Better than fine, actually. Amazing."

"Yeah, wait a minute, who are you, exactly?" Jason interrupted, glancing at her in the rear-view mirror. "Dawes? What's that? And red hair," he added thoughtfully. "I dunno if I trust red hair."

"Scarlet Dawes, but I don't know anything about her, either," Jasmine shrugged. Scarlet managed a short, nervous laugh.

"A scientist, I guess," Evolet came to the rescue. "Apparently on our side, and she came up with something for T6. What did you call it again, Miss Dawes?"

"T6S—Stabilizer," Scarlet answered simply.

Jason sighed. "That doesn't tell us anything about you, Miss Dawes!—Where are you from? Got anyone in your family? What's the white streak for? Why are you on our side? Of course, the last is the least important question of all, it's much more imperative to know why you look like that..." The older adult's slightly unhinged comments died away as he muttered them to himself quieter and quieter, until finally nobody could hear them anymore.

"From the United States, I guess," Scarlet returned slowly.

"Which of the disunited states?" Evolet pressed, with an attempt at a bit of sarcasm.

Scarlet turned slightly to look at him. "Kansas. You guys are from Maryland, right?"

"Right," Jasmine nodded.

"Background?" Evolet queried, muttering something about how Scarlet seemed to already know everything there was to know about them.

Scarlet took a deep breath. "Well, I grew up in Kansas. I'm nineteen now and I have two older brothers, David and Washington. I'm the youngest. My mom and dad were both really smart people, and... I finished high school five years ago, so my dad started letting me help in his laboratory. A year or so ago I finished college and started looking for a job. I filled out an application for Doctor Schwann's Eternity Labs, which got accepted, so... Here I am," she finished, leaning back in her seat with a slight pink flush in her cheeks.

After a moment of silence, Jasmine applauded. "Scarlet, that's really cool!"

"Thanks." The young woman smiled self-consciously.

"So, what are you going to do now?" Evolet asked slowly, putting his feet up on the seat where his sister was sitting.

Jasmine turned around to glare at him. "Stop it!"

"I dunno," Scarlet mumbled, losing her smile. "I wasn't exactly planning on throwing my career out the window like that." She glanced out the actual car window, but saw only her reflection.

Evolet sat up after a moment or so more of bothering his sister, and looked intently at the red-haired scientist. "So...you're staying with us?"

"Ha, I don't know!" Scarlet laughed. She glanced at Jasmine. "Can I?"

"Why are you asking me?" Jasmine demanded, grinning. "I'm the youngest adult in here, after all!"

"Well, we can figure that out once we get to Mexico," Jason called out from the front.

"Hospital first, please," Jasmine muttered, then winked at Scarlet. "Can't wait to hear what they say about your first-aid!"

* * *

Unfortunately Jasmine didn't keep up the same lilting spirit throughout the rest of the long drive to Mexico. They did indeed stop at a hospital, where her hand was inspected by a grave, gray-haired doctor who only looked more grave as he did some work on it. He was slightly disturbed when the anesthetic didn't work well on his patient, but he finally finished, bandaging her hand with a strict injunction for her to not use or bang it up in any way.

"Young lady, that's some serious damage and I need you to realize that," he'd told her agonizingly slowly, while peeling off his gloves and dropping them carefully into a biohazard disposal bin. "If your hand's ever going to be good for anything again, you need to keep that in mind until it's fully healed. At this point it looks like you're definitely going to end up with its being useless, at least partially. Do you understand?"

Jasmine had stared at him blankly out of long-lashed light blue eyes. "Yeah. Understood."

She, Evolet, and Scarlet marched out of the hospital, after that and after paying their bill. Evolet couldn't help but notice as they went back to the car that Jasmine still hadn't quite recovered her normally cheerful and sarcastic demeanor.

He made an attempt at a joke as he pulled the van side door open for her. "Gonna be a southpaw now, hey?"

She fixed him with a deadly glare of fury. "I'll southpaw you if you don't look out, Evolet Whyte."

And on that cheerful note, they finished the drive to Mexico, with Jason, Scarlet, and Evolet taking shifts for the actual driving. Jasmine demanded to be allowed to take a turn a few times, but naturally they wouldn't let her, which only made her grow more silent and drawn into herself in that seat of hers.

Only once did Scarlet hear her say something, and it wasn't exactly what the scientist was hoping to hear.

Jasmine shook her head glumly, staring at her bandaged right hand. "Never going to be good for anything again."

forty

"This is the address, eh?" Evolet remarked, pulling into the driveway of a rather large, albeit ordinary-looking, mansion located slightly off the outskirts of Mexico City. "Well, cool."

It was early the next afternoon, and at this point everyone was eager to be out of the van. The four kids were chatting excitedly—and restlessly—in the back seat, Jasmine was asleep in the middle seat, Scarlet was next to her, Jason was wide awake in the passenger seat, and Evolet was driving. For the last hour or so he'd been guided by an address sent him by Moira, who had succeeded in finding a house in Mexico almost immediately upon arriving with Violet and Conner. The other van had already arrived, and Evolet was slightly surprised to see Moira's Violet Army motorbike on the lawn.

"Where'd that spring from!"

Jason chuckled. "Alison took it along. Otherwise there'd probably be some drastic consequences when we walk in the door."

Evolet smiled wryly. "Yeah, I'll bet."

He shifted the van into park, and leaned back in his seat, breathing a long, relieved sigh. "Well, we're here."

Cheers from the back, and the four children immediately headed for the van doors. Laughing, Scarlet jerked the door open and hopped out, stretching. Jason got out of the passenger seat, and watched the kids tumble out one by one. He grinned.

"Your T6S works, it appears, Miss Dawes!"

She giggled delightedly. "I guess so!"

"Wake up Jaz, will you, Evy?" Jason inquired, glancing anxiously into the van. "I don't think it's a good idea to leave her there…"

"Dangerous not to," Evolet muttered. He climbed begrudgingly into the van, only to emerge rather suddenly a moment or so later, with an exclamation of "OW!"

"Leave me alone!" Jasmine shouted after him as her eyes flew open and she took in her surroundings. "Oh—oh—oh. Fine then. Whatever."

Minutes later, the Foleys, Whytes, and accompanying children were heading inside the building, Scarlet holding her folder tightly and straightening her jacket to look more grown-up. The door was opened by Moira, who straightaway grabbed Evolet and hugged him tightly. His words of protest were quickly drowned out by Jasmine's voice as she suddenly turned cheerful and threw her arms around her mother, grinning exuberantly.

"Mom!" She grinned enthusiastically, being careful to avoid crushing her hand.

"Jasmine!" Violet returned, hugging her daughter before pushing her away to look her over. Violet's face filled with alarm. "What happened to you?"

Jasmine glanced at her mother in turn. Her expression didn't change, but as she took in her mother's white, exhausted-looking face and graying hair, something died in Jasmine's eyes. "Nothing really—"

"Mom, she's pulling one over on you," Evolet broke in, having finally managed to retrieve himself from his aunt's grip. "She got shot—and cut—and—ow!"

Jasmine returned her foot to its original position, allowing a slight smirk to creep over her face. "Really though, Mom, I'm fine."

"I'm sure you are," Violet laughed. She smiled proudly at her youngest daughter, and laughed again. "Yeah, Jasmine, I'm sure you are."

Meanwhile Moira collected the four new children and rounded them off to "play" with the others in the living room. Conner showed up, shook hands with Evolet and Jason, and offered to give them all a tour—and then his gaze lit on Scarlet.

"Oh, hello," he smiled. Like Violet's, his hair was turning gray, but his welcoming expression was much like his normal self, even if Scarlet didn't know that. "Who are you?"

Taking a deep breath, Scarlet stepped forward quickly and shook the adult's hand confidently, though she could feel her knees shaking a little. "Scarlet Dawes of Eternity Labs. Nice to meet you, Mr.—Whyte?" she added hesitantly.

"Oh, yes." Conner nodded, smiling. "Nice to meet you, too. I—er—"

"She's a scientist lady we ran into at Doctor Schwann's place," Evolet broke in, much to the relief of both parties. He grinned at Conner and Scarlet both. "In fact I think she has something for the rest of the kids. What did you call it, Miss Dawes?"

"T6 Stabilizer, and call me Scarlet," Scarlet told him briefly. She glanced back at Conner then, and bit her lip nervously. "Who's in charge around here?"

"To be honest, I think that's Moira," Conner admitted, glancing around. "Moira... Moira? Where are you!"

* * *

"Okay, and now for a council of war, now that the kids are taken care of," Moira declared, hours later when the kids were in bed, all of them having been given T6S. It had been a struggle to get the excited children into bed, but superhuman adults seemed pretty capable of the job, and finally the task was accomplished; Michael and the other boys in one room, and the girls in another.

Having given them about half an hour to go to sleep, Moira, Violet, Conner, Petyr, Flynn, Jason, Tina, Scarlet, Evolet, Alison, Jasmine, and Charles convened in the dining room for a meeting, Charles having been included only after arguing that he was sixteen now, after all.

It was long past dusk outside—after ten o'clock—and the twelve adults would well have liked to go to bed as well, but they had to get this done first.

The first matter of affairs was, understandably, finding seats. There were only eight at the table and no one wanted to claim those, so Evolet immediately directed himself and Charles in the direction of one window seat. Alison and Jasmine took the other, and that left enough seats at the table for the older adults.

Scarlet pulled hers away from the table, to the wall between the window seats. She'd left her folder somewhere, probably in the room Moira had said she could share with Alison and Jasmine. Now she sat quietly, staring down at her lap as she twisted her fingers together.

Evolet watched her curiously, noticing how the tiny bit of light in the room from a lamp in the corner made the scientist look mysterious. Then Moira turned the main lights on before sitting down, and everyone could see each other clearly.

Violet was sitting next to her siblings the Foleys—she'd gradually been getting closer and closer to them since the discovery a couple of years before that they were related—and some of her old defiant spirit showed through as she dropped her fist on the table decisively.

"Alright, so what's the gameplay?"

Evolet and Jasmine looked up, realizing they hadn't yet told her about Major Lucius Arcilla's threats. But before they could say anything, Jason had a response of his own.

"I don't think we really have to do anything. We got everyone away from them safely, and... What more is there to do? We're not in the United States anymore. If we all get Mexican citizenship—"

"Wouldn't they follow us?" Charles interjected wonderingly.

Petyr shook his head confidently. "No, they can't do that—"

"Something you guys ought to know," Evolet broke in nervously, "is that their leader—not Doctor Schwann—is out for you, Mom and Dad." He bit his lip before continuing, and ran his hands through his thick brown hair. "He seemed desperate."

"What?" Violet and Conner asked sharply, both at the same time. Despite the gravity of the matter, they both looked at each other then, and Violet hid a smile.

"I mean he—Major Lucius Arcilla—wanted to find out where you'd gone," Jasmine continued for her brother, twisting her light brown hair slowly around the index finger of her left hand. "And when I say 'wanted' I mean insisted, very emphatically so. He—"

"No, it wasn't because the government wanted to know where you'd gone," Evolet cut in, sensing what the next question would be. "He had a personal quarrel of his own."

Conner glanced around. "Well, we're in Mexico now, not the United States. Arcilla can't do anything about that, can he?"

"He seemed pretty determined." Jasmine shook her head. "I don't think it really matters where we are, if he finds out."

"Something else we have to keep in mind," Moira broke in sharply, having watched the beginning of the discussion in pensive silence.

Everyone turned to look at her, but Moira was more than used to being thought of as an authority now. "We need to realize that we are fighting in two ways here—to keep away from those scientists and Major Arcilla—and then to keep the general attitude of the population on our side, wherever we go."

Everyone stared at her in surprise, and Moira laughed shortly. "Don't you see? Not everyone approves of our existence, and they've been waging a propaganda war against us ever since superhumans became a thing."

"But we won the Purple Blitzkrieg," Charles put in confusedly. "And not many people seem to hate us anymore. What do you mean?"

"I mean that until now we were on the side of the government," Moira explained patiently, something flickering in her deep blue eyes. "We were on the side of America—of peace and prosperity. But now…"

She drew her fingers across the table slowly, staring down. "Now it may look like *we* are the bad guys."

"But we aren't!" Flynn shouted, ignoring her older brother's quickly whispered warning to remain calm. "We're good guys now. We *all* are. Everyone can see that. Can't they?"

"I'm sure they could, until we unknowingly fought and won against a group of children—and then attacked a laboratory." Evolet responded almost bitterly. "I see what you mean, Aunt Moira."

Conner nodded gravely. "And that may give Major Lucius Arcilla exactly what he wants. This may be more serious than we thought."

"Obviously it is," Moira returned quickly. She looked up again, at everyone.

"We can win physical wars. We've been able to before, multiple times. But propaganda is what forced Conner, Violet, Alison, Jasmine, and Charles to live in Iceland," she reminded them softly.

"And if Major Arcilla succeeds in turning propaganda against us, especially worldwide, we can't stay here," Tina reflected aloud. "He'd find a way to follow us, and with general approval, too." She frowned. "Is there anything we can do to counteract that?"

Violet stood up then, gripping the back of her chair. "If that's the case, we have to attack them *now*, before they can attack us," she told everyone around the table, her face tight. "If we strike at the Major now, he can't follow us wherever we go next, can he?"

"No, no, Vi, we can't do that," Conner broke in. "That would be giving his confederates exactly what they need. Even if they aren't originally on his side, everyone will agree we are dangerous if we do something like that." Everyone nodded in agreement.

"But otherwise it's like a ticking time bomb," Violet insisted. "Right under our feet. Even if people are on our side now, the news media will brainwash them! We have to act now."

Her younger brother Petyr got up as well. Tall and strong, he was a T5, about the exact opposite of what Violet looked and felt like at the moment. He addressed the entire gathering. "What do we do if we don't act now? Just stay here?"

"For the time being, I guess," Conner decided, and Moira nodded her approval in turn.

"Then why don't we take a vote?" Petyr asked, shrugging. "And agree to act on it together?"

"Okay," Moira agreed, pulling out a piece of paper and a pencil. Whether from weariness or defeat, Violet sat back down, refusing to meet anyone's gaze. Conner reached across the table, and took her hand gently; she squeezed it back as a matter of course.

"Everyone who votes for immediate action, raise your hands," Moira announced. She raised her eyebrows as four hands in all went up. Violet's, Petyr's, Flynn's, and Alison's.

"I guess that decides it?" she asked after a brief pause. Slowly the hands dropped.

"I still think we're going to regret this," Violet murmured, but no one really acknowledged the fact that she'd spoken. Obviously the fact that she was the former leader of the Violet Army wasn't a good factor in the voting decision, even though pretty much everyone trusted her completely now.

"Good—if that's decided, then we just stay here for now, I suppose," Tina reflected. "When's bedtime?"

forty-one

Later that night, Scarlet was still awake.

She hadn't taken any part in the conversation and voting, partly because she felt she wasn't in any position to be making decisions with the others. She was a new person in the group, and didn't know anyone half as well as they knew each other. Having decided that, she figured she'd let events flow and stay on the better side of them, whatever that might be.

She was tired, she realized—she ought to go to sleep. But she wasn't ready to fall asleep, not quite yet. First of all, she was in a new place, with new surroundings, and even with the light turned off, she was still distracted.

And she was worried about her family. What would *they* think?

They would've heard about their daughter's actions by now, she realized glumly. Scarlet wondered exactly how the information had been presented to them—most likely by enemies, or at least people who wouldn't understand her motives. Her parents were likely hurt and confused, hearing about their daughter's traitorous defection.

Scarlet bit her lip. Her phone was on the nightstand, on airplane mode and powered off. Jason had made them all do that when they were passing through New Mexico, as a precaution. Scarlet was tempted to go turn it on and try to contact her family, but she dismissed the thought. If she did anything, there was sure to be some brilliant hacker out there who would completely decode the message and find out the sender's location.

Scarlet sighed. She felt so *useless.*

But that was when she heard the voices.

She wasn't yet used to amplified hearing, and so little things like that would keep her awake for quite a long time. Scarlet lay there and shut her eyes, hoping desperately to fall asleep soon, but in vain. She could only vaguely hear what the conversation was about, though—

But then she was quite certain she heard her name mentioned.

Scarlet sat bolt upright, realizing she'd almost fallen asleep.

For a moment her breathing came fast and hard; then she remembered where she was and almost giggled in relief. Sometimes she had nightmares like this.

The people were still talking, Scarlet realized; she frowned, slipping out of bed. She was still in her clothes. Scarlet's family didn't change to go to sleep, or at least Scarlet didn't, so she was always ready to go anywhere or do anything. Normally it would've been impossible for Scarlet to sneak out without the other superhumans in the room hearing her, but if Scarlet's hearing was amplified so were her other senses, and she made her way out quietly enough to avoid waking the others.

Stepping into the hallway, she followed the voices to—the kitchen.

She walked into the middle of...a midnight conference? Violet and Moira had been talking; as Scarlet approached, they both fell silent, standing up.

Scarlet stood in the kitchen doorway. For a moment the three regarded each other silently, and Scarlet couldn't help but notice that Moira and Violet were both completely dressed, as if they were going somewhere.

"Oh, hello, Miss Dawes," Moira greeted her finally, though her eyes were narrowed. "Trouble sleeping?"

Scarlet nodded. "Yeah. Is there any water around here?"

"Yeah, I'll get you some," Moira nodded, turning and leading the way into the darkened kitchen.

Behind them, Violet turned to leave. "We'll continue this conversation later, Moira," she called crisply. Scarlet heard her march out, something hard and decisive in her footsteps.

* * *

The next day dawned about six hours later, though no one really got up until eight o'clock. Scarlet was among the early risers, however; and she was surprised to find Jasmine in the girls' bathroom with the door open, trying to change her bandage over the sink with one hand. It was hard going, and she looked up and sighed as Scarlet stood in the doorway.

"Morning. 'Sup?"

Scarlet slipped into the tile-floored room, brushing her red hair energetically. "Just life. Want help?"

"Sure, but finish that first," Jasmine told her, managing a grin. Scarlet smiled back, shutting the door.

Shrugging, Scarlet swung her hair out in front of her, standing at the mirror. She saw the white streak, and paused, frowning; then sighed hopelessly. Her hair had gone on a growth spurt after her injection, and the new white section was about an inch long—and wasn't showing any signs of disappearing.

But of course it wouldn't disappear overnight, she reminded herself.

"It'll take time," Jasmine told her, as if she were reading her mind.

Scarlet nodded, and forced a smile. "Yeah."

Reaching up and quickly drawing her hair into a high ponytail, Scarlet turned with a flourish. "Okay. Let's see about that hand of yours."

"There are some more bandages in the cabinet, if you need them," Jasmine told her. She considered sitting down on the counter, but then realized Scarlet probably wouldn't be able to easily reach her that way.

"Right. And what about your shoulder?" Scarlet raised her eyebrows.

Jasmine shrugged carelessly. "I can do that on my own, I think."

"If you insist," Scarlet sighed.

Quickly but carefully, she began undoing the bandages on Jasmine's right hand. The deeper layers were soaked in half-dried blood, but at least her hand had stopped bleeding eventually, and Scarlet finally managed to get the wrappings off without starting the hand bleeding again. She stared at it, and shook her head in dismay.

"It's scarring," she told Jasmine, who had her eyes tightly shut. "But it doesn't look good."

Jasmine opened her eyes then. "Oh, *bother*," she sighed. "Just wrap it up again, I guess. New bandages, of course," she added hastily.

"Well, I would assume," Scarlet laughed, trying to relieve some of the stress. Even though she had taken first aid classes, there was always only so much blood and injury she could handle before it became repugnant.

"Yeah, what am I thinking?" Jasmine continued the game. "You're not one of my brothers. You're not Evolet."

"Would Evolet really do that?" Scarlet asked, wide-eyed.

Jasmine laughed. "Ha, no. I was being sarcastic. You'll pick it up if you stay with us."

She winked, and Scarlet laughed.

"Guess so."

forty-two

What the two young ladies didn't know was that in the early hours of the morning, Violet had left. It was an impromptu decision, hastened by her conference with Moira around midnight.

She had gone back to her room with something of her old energy after Scarlet interrupted the conversation. Now Violet sat down heavily on the bed, breathing hard.

There were shadows of fatigue under her eyes, and she sighed loudly, thinking hard as she ran her hands through her graying brown hair in a way much like Evolet would.

Though there was no one in the room to see it, her eyes were flashing. Violet bit her lip until it bled.

She stood up suddenly, and went over to the dresser in the room, opening the top drawer and pulling out a purple jacket. Looking at it for a moment in the dim light of a lamp, she unzipped one of the pockets, and slipped her hand into it.

Her hand emerged a moment later, this time with two vials in its palm.

Violet stared at them for a moment.

One vial she replaced in her pocket; the other she gripped tightly as she retrieved one of the paradraline kits from a closet in the hallway.

She emptied a syringe into the bathroom sink, and then refilled it with the liquid from one of her vials. Jerking the vial off the needle and tossing it into the trashcan, she sat down on her bed and looked at the medical implement for a moment. The purple color was strange in the dim light.

Violet took a deep breath, then winced as she began to inject herself.

She gasped as a reaction began, but she didn't stop.

Her grip strengthened within seconds.

Smiling, Violet stood up and threw away the vial, slowly putting on the purple jacket. The fatigue was gone from her face.

She was herself again.

* * *

The household didn't know anything about Violet's disappearance until around noon, when finally a committee of children was sent to fetch her for lunch. They returned excitedly bearing an envelope labeled *Only for Conner and Moira.*

Moira read it first, and her brow furrowed in puzzlement and annoyance as she handed it to Conner, shaking her head. He read it and sat down weakly, closing his eyes. Everyone stared at Moira expectantly.

"She's gone off and left," Moira explained finally, heading into the kitchen to dish out lunch.

As no more information was forthcoming, everyone except Conner followed her, clamoring with questions. Finally Moira resorted to grabbing a wooden spoon and whacking—T4-ified people wouldn't take too much damage from one of those, would they?

"Out!" she shouted, exasperated. "Everybody out except Evolet and the adults!"

Finally, after a few hectic moments, the children had been banished, and Moira finished making lunch preparations. She moved with hard precision. Petyr, Flynn, Jason, Tina, Scarlet, and Evolet were in the room. The other three women set about pouring cups of orange juice for the kids; Petyr, Jason, and Evolet found themselves trying and failing miserably to look like they were being useful.

Moira glanced over them once or twice, with very obvious thoughts of kicking them all out, but the urgency of the situation prevailed, and soon she was explaining further.

"Violet has decided that if we all stay here we're simply waiting for the

Major to find us," she told them all seriously, pulling the macaroni and cheese out of the oven. "She's decided to head them off and try to rid us of the danger as well, by finding out where they're keeping Schwann3 and destroying it. She says that way we can all be safe."

Evolet's jaw dropped. "Mom—how? Literally *how* can she do this, Aunt Moira?" he questioned in disbelief. "She's—"

Moira turned to look hard at him. "She said she has T4 again. Now, what I want to know is—"

She was interrupted by half a dozen startled exclamations. "How on earth?" Evolet demanded, and the expressions on the older adults' faces spoke much the same reaction. Scarlet's blue eyes widened in shock.

"That's *exactly* what I want to know," Moira continued briefly. "But it's too late to deal with that now. Someone has got to go after her and stop her. The way she was talking to me last night—she doesn't expect to be coming back. But—"

She hesitated, her deep blue eyes blinking. "I don't think we are ready to lose her yet, any of us. And she can't do something like destroy Schwann3—not by herself. Someone is going to have to help her. I know your dad would, Evolet, but he physically *can't*. Violet wants me to do something else, so someone has to stay here to help look after the kids—"

"I'll go find Mom," Evolet volunteered immediately. "I know Jasmine will, too."

Moira nodded, and something faded in her eyes as she looked away from her eldest nephew. "Tina and Flynn, can you stay here? I have to do something for Violet, and Ali can't watch seven superhuman kids on her own. I should know that," she added with a humorless chuckle and a sideways glance at Evolet, who grinned slightly. "Jason and Petyr—you'll help Evolet and Jasmine, won't you?"

"And so will I," Scarlet put in suddenly from her quiet little corner. "I'll go with them."

Moira glanced at her in surprise. "You will?"

"Yes, but one stipulation—I need to talk to my family as well, sometime during this trip," Scarlet told her, fidgeting. "But yeah, I'll help them. If I can," she added, muttering.

"You can," Evolet assured her, smiling. Scarlet returned the smile half-heartedly.

Something suspiciously like a twinkle showed in Moira's eyes as she watched them. "Well, is that settled?" she asked everyone decisively a moment later. "Let's get to it, then."

forty-three

"You know, Evolet, I'm afraid," Jasmine confided to her older brother a few hours later, once she, Scarlet, and he were in one of the vans. Petyr and Jason were taking the other one, since they'd decided to split up, and Moira had her motorcycle.

Evolet had been consulting a map—no one was supposed to turn on cell phones until they were past a certain distance from the house—but now he looked up and glanced at Jasmine, who was sitting in the passenger seat—Scarlet was in the row of seats behind them. Jasmine's light blue eyes met his purple ones meaningfully, and he frowned.

"Afraid of what?" he asked slowly. Scarlet seemed preoccupied.

Jasmine bit her lip, staring down at her still-bandaged hand. "Is Aunt Moira telling us everything?"

"I dunno," Evolet admitted, shrugging and starting the car engine. "Why?"

"I mean, she told us Mom wants to head the Major off and away from us, but if that was all, then why would Moira be sending us after her?" Jasmine pointed out. "That...defeats the purpose."

"Maybe she's worried about her," Evolet suggested, but his sister shook her head.

"No, it wouldn't be just that. If Mom has T4 again, she can take care of herself," Jasmine asserted confidently. "But Aunt Moira told us... Aunt Moira told us to *stop* her."

Evolet took a deep breath, moving the van controls out of park position and letting it roll slowly down the hill.

"That doesn't mean anything more," he returned, taking one hand off the steering wheel to run it through his hair—and then hurriedly replacing it in something like panic.

Jasmine groaned. "Evolet, why don't you get what I'm saying?" she asked hopelessly. "I don't want to say it…"

"Fine." Evolet sighed. "I don't know."

"I think she's trying to say that your aunt is worried that your mother may have other motives than simply leading them off," Scarlet spoke up suddenly from behind them.

Startled, Evolet glanced in the rearview mirror, and saw she was looking straight at it as well—at him.

Keeping the eye contact, the young scientist went on: "For example, if I as an outsider were to hear about a laboratory being destroyed by a former terrorist leader, I'd immediately connect it to the terrorist's war."

She bit her lip. "Even if that's not what your mother is intending."

Evolet's mouth dropped open. "But—no!" he fairly shouted. "No! Mom would never do anything like that again. She's changed. She wouldn't. Or… *would* she?"

He glanced at Jasmine, his eyes full of horror. She didn't meet his gaze.

"Well, naturally you guys would know her better than I would," Scarlet amended quickly. "Just saying. That's what I'd think as an outsider."

"Well, please don't," Evolet told her, "because you aren't an outsider anymore." Without another word, he guided the van down the long driveway towards the road.

No, Violet would not be starting another Purple Blitzkrieg. Evolet told himself that over and over again. She had completely changed now. No matter what the government might do to them, Violet wasn't going to do something like that again. Moira had told him that, even if Violet hadn't herself. Violet would obviously try to protect her family, but as for taking revenge on the government—

His face twisted as he remembered the look of doubt on Moira's face when she read the note, and Evolet wondered if she really believed Violet was good as completely as she'd told Evolet. Evolet shook his head. No, Violet was good. She'd reformed, after all. She had no thoughts of starting another war.

But even as he told himself those things, Evolet was seized with a panic. They had to find Violet and stop her, right away!

If the government got the impression Scarlet had suggested, they would either kill her in combat or execute her, without listening to explanations. Evolet knew right away that he had to find his mother and protect her. He would give her the benefit of the doubt. She could explain why she was doing this, and he knew she would. Everything would be fine. They were going to find Violet, maybe help her to destroy Schwann3, and then throw that horrible Major off their tracks, and go somewhere safe.

Yet, in the back of his mind, there was still that flicker of doubt, no matter how hard he tried to shake it off. Evolet hated it. Why couldn't he just *believe* that his mother was good?

"Evolet?" he heard, as if in a dream, and suddenly realized Jasmine had been calling his name as she reached across with her left hand and tapped his shoulder. "Hello? Earth to Evolet?"

"What?" The twenty-year-old jumped, startled. In the back seat, Scarlet laughed aloud, and Jasmine repressed a smile.

"Where are we going?" Jasmine asked him again, with a look of long-suffering patience.

"Oh…good question," Evolet admitted, realizing he was just driving down the street. "Can you get the GPS started?"

* * *

That night, Moira left as well. She had another destination entirely, as would have been noticed had anyone seen her arrive at the airport and board a plane for England. Before the plane took off, she took out her phone, turned it on for the first time in over twenty-four hours, and called someone.

"I'm leaving now. Where are you?" she asked hastily, as soon as the other person accepted the call. Moira glanced around discreetly, but thankfully no one seemed to be watching her.

"Two hours away from Eternity Labs," came the muffled answer. "You?"

"At the airport," Moira returned. "In the plane, I mean. I'll text you the coordinates when I find them, okay?"

"Okay."

"Oh, and another thing—your kids and siblings are on their way," Moira added, smiling briefly to herself. "You can't do this alone, Vi. See you soon."

"Moira—" and that was all Moira could hear before she hung up and replaced her phone in her pocket.

At the other end of the abruptly ended call, Violet's thoughts had turned nearly as purple as her name and eyes, though Moira wouldn't have been able to see those even if she had been there. Violet was driving a small blue five-seater, wearing her bulletproof purple jacket as she had in the years before her Schwann3 injection. Those jackets were practically a symbol of her family now, and she smiled at the thought as some of her anger dissipated.

"You just don't trust me," she told Moira aloud, despite the fact that she was alone. "But why'd you have to get the kids in danger? Though I guess they would've insisted on it, themselves."

Violet smiled fondly.

Evolet would've been the first, I know it.

I'll just have to finish before they arrive.

forty-four

Two days later, at Eternity Labs, Major Lucius Arcilla had heard through his intelligence that the superhumans were on their way to the Texas laboratory.

The Major was grimly satisfied. He'd been thinking he'd have to hunt for them—and here they were, coming straight to him. His unusual happiness showed through as he gave his commands to his subordinates.

"We'll be having visitors soon. Now, there's only two ways they can get in here—over the fence, or from the air," he asserted confidently. "I want men posted along the fence, and we'll be watching the skies. I expect our visitors will be trying to get their hands on Schwann3, so I'm going to send samples of it to Washington, see?" He smiled. "Also, let's get all the cameras in perfect working order. I want video documentation."

He was in charge now, since Eternyti Schwann had been in med bay since the first attack—in intensive care, too. She was definitely in no position to be giving orders, and so Lucius was the main authority at Eternity Labs for the moment. So everyone settled down to wait for the expected combat.

Nothing happened all day, which didn't surprise the Major. But then nothing happened all night, and Lucius finally went to bed around 4AM, puzzled and let down. Where *were* they?

He found that out about four hours later, being forcefully awakened by a blaring alarm from the hallway. Throwing on his uniform and muttering under his breath, Lucius dashed out into the hall, shouting orders into his walkie-talkie as he went. The alarm kept going. "Intruder alert: unauthorized entry to Lab 01. Intruder alert..."

"Lock the building down!" Lucius roared, shoving past confused personnel on his way to the door. "Shut down the laboratories!"

He grabbed hold of one of his men and shook him. "How'd they get in here?"

The man shook his head, stuttering. "I don't know—not the fence, that's for sure—there was a delivery half an hour ago—"

"Blast!" Lucius muttered, letting him go and continuing on his way to the laboratory building. "Of *course!*"

* * *

If Lucius wanted the laboratory building locked down, he certainly got what he wanted. In Lab 01, Violet had carefully secured the door behind her before tossing her glasses, cap, and delivery-truck jacket onto an empty table. There was no one else in the room, but if there had been Violet would definitely have taken care of them before retrieving a couple of large, *Fragile*-marked packages from the bag she carried and setting them on the table as well.

Leaving them there, she glanced up momentarily at a red, blinking security camera in a corner of the room, and then shrugged, ignoring it as she stepped across the room with a lively spring in her step, looking at the labels on the cabinets and pulling on latex gloves at the same time.

Finally, at about the same time as yelling began in the hallway, she found the cabinet she was looking for. Smiling grimly, despite the muffled shouts from outside the room, Violet tried to pull the cabinet open, only to discover it was locked. Her smile changed to a frown, and she tugged it violently, but it didn't open.

Biting her lip, Violet stared hard at the reinforced metal box, and then glanced around the room as if for inspiration. Just then, a voice came through on the speakers in the ceiling.

"Violet Whyte, you are surrounded—and on camera. Walk to the middle of the room, disarm yourself, and hold your hands over your head. Follow those instructions immediately, or else we will not hesitate to use weapons."

An amused smile flitted across Violet's face as she listened. She didn't know Major Arcilla's voice, but she was willing to bet this deep, harsh one belonged to him. She looked around searchingly for a moment, and her eyes rested on a couple of lockers set in the opposite wall. Still ignoring Lucius's threat, Violet leaped over to the wall, slamming her hand down on a button.

The lockers slid open, revealing rows of masks complete with oxygen tanks. Violet grabbed one, fitting it over her nose and mouth just as a pale green gas slowly began to sift out from dispensers in the ceiling.

Quickly strapping the respiratory device on securely, the superhuman walked back to the cabinet, then quickly to another section of the room where she found a drawerful of implements.

Violet Whyte, née Arnnu or Foley, hadn't grown up around laboratories for no reason. Locating a specific type of knife relatively quickly, she walked back over to the cabinet as the room fogged over. Violet glanced at the knife, holding it carefully.

Taking a deep breath, she stabbed it into the metal door of the cabinet, sawing downwards. Seconds later she could reach into the box, and she did so, grabbing a half-empty container of syringes and pulling it back out in her latex-gloved hand. The machine beeped when she grabbed the box, but Violet ignored that. Her glove was torn against the jagged metal, and some of her skin too, but Violet didn't care about that either, and rushed the syringes over to the table with the mail packages.

Tearing open the packages, Violet unceremoniously dumped them out on the table. Two syringes fell out of each one. Snatching them up, she flipped open the syringes container and replaced the four new syringes in some of the empty slots.

She went hunting among the cabinets again, a task which was harder this time because of the green fog. But finally she found what she was looking for, and ran back over to the table to fetch the syringes. Then she opened the container and shook the syringes out—into a vat of acid.

The acid hissed and fumed, eating through the plastic containers. Then it consumed the Schwann3 that had been inside the syringes; the acid turned red, fizzing violently. Eventually, however, the red dispersed, leaving only the pale yellow smoke to creep upward and merge with the green. The acid grew still.

Violet stood back, and watched the yellow smoke, which was the last remaining component of Schwann3. She took a deep breath, ignoring the sounds of the door being knocked down.

Her mission here was complete.

forty-five

I t was about then that Evolet and Jasmine arrived in the van. Scarlet had gone to find a helicopter, and right now Evolet and Jasmine were banking on the hope that the laboratory security would let them in.

Bringing the van to a stop, Evolet couldn't help but notice that the security man who ran up to them looked completely confused and scared.

He waved at him tentatively. "Hey there—can I drive in?"

"Who are you?" the guard asked, staring at the purple-eyed twenty-year-old.

"Evolet and Jasmine Whyte," Evolet identified quickly; and before they could interrupt him, he went on with: "We're here to help. Mom is here and we need to stop her—she is here, right?"

The officer's eyes widened. "Yes, she's here. But I'm not sure if I can let you in—"

"Near enough is good enough," Evolet grinned—and the van shot forward suddenly, just missing the startled official and tearing through the blockade. The man ran after the speeding van for a few seconds, then gave up, staring dismally as he pulled out his walkie-talkie and began talking into it quickly.

"A miss is as good as a mile!" Jasmine yelled through her window.

Evolet kept on pushing the van, down the driveway and then off the driveway towards one of the buildings around which soldiers were crowding. Finally bringing the vehicle to a halt, he jumped out, immediately being surrounded by soldiers who had their guns out and at the ready. Jasmine found herself in the same position.

"What's the deal?" Evolet asked, watching them levelly, his back to the van. "We're here to help."

"Hands up," one told him severely, looking at him out of steely eyes.

After a moment of hesitation, Evolet slowly raised his hands over his head, still smiling, though it was forced at this point. Someone prodded him with their gun, and he jumped slightly.

"Who are you?" the spokesman asked, but answered himself before Evolet could. "You're Evolet Whyte. Here to help, eh? You can tell that to the Major—"

"No, I'm not joking," Evolet broke in impatiently, his own eyes narrowing. "Mom's here and only Jaz and I can stop her. You need to let us pass," he told the man seriously. "Now."

"You aren't fooling us," the soldier returned. He beckoned to the young adult. "Come with us."

"Take me to the Major," Evolet returned. "Jaz and me. We'll talk to him. He'll let us help, you'll see." Evolet wasn't so sure that the Major would let them help, but he decided to stay confident. At this point, confidence was all he had.

* * *

"Your mother was just in our laboratories, destroying the place. T4 again, I see. This wouldn't be happening if you'd told me where she was," Lucius told Evolet as soon as the two Whytes were brought into his office and the door closed on them, leaving only Evolet, Jasmine, and Lucius. The Major ignored Jasmine, who stood behind Evolet, scowling at the Major whenever she got the chance.

Evolet ignored the Major's verbal attack. "Do you want our help or not? We can get Mom to stop, but we aren't going to unless you promise she'll get a trial and everything."

Evolet smiled slightly. In a trial, everything would be exposed—Schwann3 and Lucius Arcilla's ulterior motives. The Whytes would be safe.

Lucius looked him over carefully, his eyes narrowing into slits. "Fine," he said finally. "But you're too late to help *here*. Last I heard, Violet Whyte was on her way out of here, borrowing a company convertible." He stood up. "I'll get you a helicopter and a pilot."

"I can fly," Evolet and Jasmine both interjected, then glanced at each other in surprise.

"I don't think Miss Whyte is in any condition to fly," Lucius pointed out dryly, as if he was just noticing it for the first time. Jasmine glared at him out of light blue eyes.

"Well, then—" Evolet began, anxious to break the tense silence.

Lucius led the way to the door. "You two will probably want to discuss plans, and besides, someone has got to fly the helicopter if you need to drop out or something. I'll find you a pilot," he repeated firmly, and swung the door open, marching out and down the hall.

Shrugging, Evolet and Jasmine followed, slightly surprised at the Major's cooperation, though the glint in Jasmine's eyes gave Evolet the impression that she wasn't completely cured of the idea of smashing the Major over the head, hard. Jasmine had a feeling she was going to regret not doing it, later.

Even though the Major had inferred very clearly that there were helicopters on the premises, Evolet and Jasmine were still surprised to be introduced to the Eternity Labs hangar, a large, one-story building which consisted mostly of garage. Inside were three small helicopters, all in prime condition.

Lucius led them towards one of them, without hesitation; halfway there, he hailed a young man who'd been leaning against the wall doing something on his phone. The man looked up.

"Here, George, I've got some passengers for you. Are you ready to fly?" the Major asked him quickly.

"Oh, yes, Major," the man returned, slipping his phone into his pocket and walking over.

"Following a company car that just left the compound, heading east and far over the speed limit," Lucius explained shortly. "Leave now with these two and try to get them on the scene. I'll follow with backup," he added, turning around and heading back out of the hangar without further ado. "Oh, and get them some intercoms!"

And then he was gone. Shrugging, George glanced momentarily over his two passengers, and then led the way towards one of the aircraft.

Once in the helicopter, George prepared for takeoff, while Evolet took the copilot's seat and Jasmine strapped herself in behind them. It was quite the feat with only one usable hand, but she managed it finally. Seeing that both his companions were ready, George flipped a switch on the control panel, and the helicopter lit up. He pressed a button, and then part of the hangar roof slid away, leaving just the open sky above them. George started the engine, and Evolet and Jasmine braced themselves.

"All clear?" George called over the engine.

"All clear!" the Whytes yelled back.

George slammed a lever home, and then a few seconds later they were airborne. Evolet couldn't help the laugh that escaped him as the helicopter rose, despite the (non)gravity of the situation. He loved flying.

"Let's help you find the car to follow," Jasmine decided, obviously talking to George. "And then I think Evy and I need to call some people. Mom—and Scarlet."

forty-six

Half an hour later, after failing to contact Violet but succeeding in calling Scarlet, Evolet and Jasmine found themselves in a new situation entirely.

They were still in the air but now so was their quarry. Violet had driven to an airport and apparently borrowed a helicopter, which made the chase now an air one. Lucius was in a helicopter as well, and presumably his soldiers as well. They were tailing George's copter, which in turn was following Violet's.

Evolet and Jasmine had tried multiple times to call their mother, but to no avail. It went to the voicemail every time.

They were going over trees now, and if the Whytes looked hard they could see a formation of caves among the trees. Evolet held his phone in his lap, tensely wondering if it would be worth trying to call Violet again—and then gunfire rang out.

He looked up, startled. Jasmine began saying something but never finished it; George muttered something.

All three of them stared ahead, out the dashboard windows.

Lucius's helicopter was shooting at the one Violet was in, and now as George, Evolet, and Jasmine watched, the helicopter veered sharply and then went into a nosedive, crippled.

The Whytes caught their breath; but then they saw the door open and Violet jump out, falling for about two seconds before releasing her parachute and drifting slowly down to the forest.

More shots rang out before Evolet or Jasmine had time to radio Lucius, and they saw Violet jerking on the parachute strings to make herself fall faster.

Evolet slammed his finger down on the PTT on his intercom. "Major, stop!" he yelled desperately. "Jaz and I are heading in!"

He released the button as Violet disappeared among the treetops. George hovered the aircraft, looking around at both of them. "What?"

"Parachute, Jaz," Evolet ordered briskly, ignoring their pilot. "Got it? Let's go."

They already had them strapped on, and now Evolet motioned to George, who opened the doors. Taking deep breaths, Evolet and Jasmine looked at each other for a moment before they jumped out—together, holding hands.

Evolet jerked the strap to release his parachute—then realized Jasmine was having trouble with hers. His parachute alone couldn't handle the weight of two of them. Quickly he jerked her cord as well, and they both began a smooth descent. Evolet had a moment to look around him.

The shooting had stopped; he was grateful for that. Now he held the PTT again as he and his younger sister floated downwards, Jasmine breathing heavily.

"Major, we're going to try and talk to Mom," he spoke into it swiftly, not waiting for an answer before he continued. "Stop shooting. I'm serious. She'll listen to us."

"You'd better be right, Evolet Whyte," came the hard return, and then the speaker fell silent.

Evolet bit his lip, feeling not for the first time compunction in teaming up with the obviously self-seeking Major. He ignored the feeling with an effort. He and Jasmine would find Violet, and they'd talk to her, and she'd agree to stop. Sure, the Major would pick them all up, but Violet would get a chance to explain herself, and all they'd have to do would be explain what Lucius and Eternyti were trying to do with Schwann3. It was illegal; he knew that, and they had plenty of witnesses.

Everything would go back to normal again, he told himself as they dropped among the trees—and almost immediately their parachutes got stuck.

Grabbing support from the forest's leafy branches, he and Jasmine cut themselves loose and began their descent—Evolet's quick and impatient, Jasmine's slow and cautious.

The end was in sight: they could both see Violet at the entryway of one of the caves, watching them while carrying a box of something.

Everything will be okay, Evolet told himself again.

* * *

Major Lucius Arcilla was having very different thoughts at the moment, as he watched the Whytes' parachutes blossom out and fall slowly to the ground. He motioned to his team of ten soldiers—all that would fit in the helicopter— and they crowded around to listen.

"We're going to be going down now, and we're going to find out where they've gone to hide, understand?" The men nodded. "Everyone should have their guns and dart-guns ready. We'll surround them, and then we'll open fire. I don't want a single one left alive, do you guys comprehend that?" he asked them, his expression hard and cold.

They nodded again, and Lucius made sure the rope mechanism was working. They'd all slide down it, one at a time, once he told the pilot to stop and open the doors.

He glanced back at his soldiers to make sure they were ready. And they were: each one carried two handguns and two dart-guns. The darts were Schwann2, the chemical compound which was lethal to T4 and T5. It was harmless against hyper-T5 and T6, but their present targets were only T4.

Though there were only eleven normal humans altogether, Lucius was confident of success. Three well-shot darts would finish the battle.

Smiling satisfiedly, Lucius walked over to the pilot without grabbing the hand-grips along the ceiling. He nodded to the man.

"Drop the rope and open the doors. We're going in."

The pilot nodded, pulling down a lever and then slamming another one home. In the main partition of the capable and lightly built aircraft, the ten soldiers watched as the doors opened and the rope slid out.

Lucius grabbed it first, and leaned out, looking up and seeing the wings flash by above him noisily. Finding a better grip, he slithered down. One by one, his men followed.

"Mom!" Evolet yelled, running towards the cave as soon as his feet hit the ground. He tripped on a branch and caught himself without losing his stride. "Mom, stop!"

Violet looked up, still in the cave entrance, from where she'd been emptying out the box's contents on the ground. She watched him running to her, and watched Jasmine jump the last few feet and start running as well.

Her long, light brown hair swirled about her in the morning wind, gray at the roots. Her face, though much more alive and much less wrinkled than when Evolet had seen her last, was wan and gray, and there was a warm sadness in her purple eyes, her eyes that matched the jacket she was wearing.

Evolet realized with a start that she was wearing her old gear—the outfit she'd worn as Violet Army leader—and the implication hit him hard.

He slowed as he approached the cave, his face working. What was she doing?

"Why are you two here?" Violet demanded, her voice strong and supreme as usual. "Shoo! Get out! This place is going to be a warzone," she added, looking beyond Evolet to where she could see the soldiers descending from their helicopter.

By now Jasmine had caught up with Evolet, though out of breath. She took in the contents of Violet's box at a glance. It was explosives, and Violet obviously intended to blow up the cave's entrance. Jasmine bit her lip as she, too, realized Violet was dressed for battle.

"Mom, we have to go," she told her, panting. "We can't fight the soldiers. This isn't the same as Ayan and Louis and Zaire and the rest. We can't fight the government, they're only doing—"

"What they think is best," Violet finished smoothly. "But so am I, and Major Arcilla isn't. Get out of here."

"Mom, please," Evolet pleaded. He glanced around and saw the soldiers who were now running through the forest underbrush, spreading out in a circle around the cave mouth. "Please don't do this—"

"Why are you working with Arcilla?" Violet broke in, shaking her head. Snapping out of her inactivity, she began positioning the explosives again. "I told you two to get out of here. Now do it!"

"They're not after us, Mom!" Jasmine shouted, running forward into the cave with her mother. Evolet followed, somewhat more slowly.

"Mom, we talked to the Major and he agreed that if we stop you then you'll get a trial." Jasmine's voice was serious. "And in a trial the truth will come out." Her light blue eyes were pleading. "Let's not fight, Mom. You got rid of all the Schwann3, didn't you? Wasn't that all you set out to do?"

Violet's purple eyes glistened, and she looked away from them both, pulling out a match. She held it a few inches away from the rocky wall of the cave, and paused. "My work here is finished. Don't make me tell you again to get out of here," she hissed, watching the soldiers.

"Mom, if we surrender we'll be fine," Evolet whispered to her, tensing, ready to catch the match.

"Back off, both of you," Violet ordered. "I'm going to collapse the cave entry, and then we're all going to get out of here—"

"Mom, we can't run forever!" Jasmine burst out. "They won't hurt us! Just let's—"

And just then she found out how wrong she was.

All at once, the soldiers opened fire. Bullets tore into the cave, most of them coming to an abrupt stop either against the Whytes' purple jackets or in the stone walls of the cave.

Evolet felt one hit his leg, just above the ankle; if anything, it helped him drop to the ground at the same time as Violet and Jasmine.

Evolet shut his eyes tightly, knowing the pain would soon pass. The three heard one or more of the soldiers utter a muffled exclamation of annoyance.

"Uhh—" Jasmine began, her voice wavering in surprise. "I—"

"Both of you get to the back," Violet hissed. "You should've listened earlier. Don't you realize that Arcilla is *using* you?"

She glanced sideways, at Evolet, and her gaze softened. "Are you okay?"

Evolet still couldn't believe what was happening. He was in a sort of shock, from pain and disbelief together, but he managed to answer the question by nodding his head.

Satisfied, Violet looked forward again as the soldiers broke cover and advanced.

She reached out—still holding the match. Violet's fingers discovered a rocky outcrop on the ground. She fumbled with the match, trying desperately to light it. She was going to collapse the entrance, and might well be buried in the process, but she knew that together, though they might be wounded, Evolet and Jasmine would be able to get her out.

Some of the anxiety disappeared from Violet's face, and she scraped the end of the match against the stone, hard.

Rssk. Violet watched the flame for a moment as it faltered at first and then grew strong, reflected in her purple eyes.

Instinctively dropping her head again as more shots rattled past, she waited for the firing to stop, and then scrambled up quickly, still holding the lit match. In an instant she was on her knees, and the match was flying towards the explosives.

And then it was shot out of the air, and the tiny light was extinguished, only moments away from its destination. Violet bit her lip, jerking the box of matches out of her pocket and beginning to retrieve another one—

Then came a shower of darts—only eleven of them, but still deadly. Violet held her breath, remaining immovable as two fell against her jacket and another lodged in a wisp of her light brown hair. Then it was over—

A hair-raising scream rang out from behind her.

Jasmine.

Jasmine.

Violet was on her feet, and so was Evolet. He got to his sister first, and Violet saw him pick up the dart and stare at it in dismay. Its tip was bloody, and even as Jasmine's scream died away Violet knew what she had to do.

She stepped over to Evolet and grabbed his shoulder as he knelt there, his hands on Jasmine's shoulders as he shouted her name and her light blue eyes closed.

Evolet looked up at Violet, his eyes glazing over with tears.

Tearing her free hand out of her pocket, she stuffed a rolled-up map into his hand, and closed his fingers around it firmly. Violet tipped her head towards the back of the cave. The shelter her children should have already reached.

Her voice was thick with fear and love, even as she shouted at him almost angrily. "Get her over there and take care of her. NOW!"

forty-eight

Evolet let go of his sister and then collapsed on the ground in the next section of the cave, breathing heavily. His foot was screaming for attention, but he didn't have time for that now. His numb fingers fumbled with the rolled-up paper. He pulled it open, letting whatever was inside fall to his lap as he glanced at Jasmine. She lay motionless where he'd left her, halfway on her side, her eyes half-open now.

Evolet looked down at his lap, seeing the small purple vial for the first time—no, it wasn't the first time, he realized. He picked it up and stared at it.

Then he knew what Violet meant—and what he had to do with it.

He found his pocketknife. Sitting back on his knees and bracing himself, he made a small cut in his younger sister's arm, biting his lip as the cut began to bleed—but that was what he needed.

Without bothering to clean the blade of his knife, he inserted the sharp tip into the lid of the syringe capsule, twisting it and then pulling it out. Quickly he turned it, dumping the serum into the cut he'd made. He dropped both the capsule and the knife then, and leaned forward, watching Jasmine anxiously as the T4 did its work—or that's what he hoped it was doing. His foot burned like fire, but that wasn't what was bothering him right now.

Jasmine was so still. He couldn't remember seeing her this still, not since the LVK when she'd been twelve. And now it was because of something else. Evolet was horribly, terribly scared. Would the T4 work? If it didn't, then Jasmine was going to die—if she hadn't already.

His eyes had already misted over, and now he began actually crying, even as the sounds of battle sounded in the first section of the cave. He was racked with sobs. Jasmine couldn't die. The two were inseparable, now. If Jasmine died—

Evolet leaned forward, gripping his leg. His tears dripped down onto Jasmine's face, and he closed his eyes. He couldn't look at her anymore.

Not Jasmine!

Evolet felt like he could go out there and tear Lucius apart with his bare hands. He probably could, too. He wanted to. But he couldn't leave his sister here.

Jasmine...

He opened his eyes, hoping against hope. His vision was blurry, and for a moment he thought she was looking up at him. He froze, and caught his breath, brushing the tears from his eyes with his purple jacket sleeve. What?

No, he was seeing things. Evolet blinked, and blinked again in shock. He stopped crying, and slowly a smile lit up his face. Jasmine's eyes were open. And she was smiling at him.

Evolet smiled until his jaw hurt. He was speechless.

And then Jasmine started laughing.

"You okay, Evy?"

"I thought you were dead!" Evolet, too, burst into nearly hysterical laughter. But then the distant shouting reminded him what was going on, and he forced himself to calm down. "A—are you feeling better?"

"Weak, but I'll live," Jasmine assured him, taking a deep breath. "Where's Mom?"

"I—" Evolet picked up the paper Violet had given to him, glanced over it, and stopped short mid-sentence. Well, at the beginning of his sentence, at least.

It was a map. A world map, with coordinates hastily scrawled on it in large handwriting, and the word *Mongolia.* Smaller, in the right-bottom corner of the map, was the message: *It's safe. Happy travels. God bless you all.*

Evolet knew his mother's handwriting, but even if he hadn't, it was obvious enough what the implication of the message was. His blood froze.

It was all just too much, too sudden.

"What?" Jasmine asked him curiously, but he wasn't listening. His mind was reeling. How could he have ever doubted his mother?

She was doing all of this for them. Re-injecting herself with T4, attacking Eternity Labs, destroying the Schwann3—for them. She had been right that they had to do something; she had been right about the Major.

Of *course* she was. Evolet felt like he was going to be sick.

His mother was doing all this for them—for him—and he'd suspected her of...acting as a terrorist!

And then suddenly it hit him that she was out there, fighting alone, for him and for Jasmine and for everyone they shared the different strains of T4 with.

It was true, T4 was thicker than water.

But so was blood—which was thicker even than T4.

No matter what else she might be, Violet was his *mother*.

Evolet stood up with a sudden snap and handed the map to Jasmine.

She looked at him sharply. "What are you doing?"

"I'm going to help Mom," Evolet gritted. "Stay here."

"Not like I can go anywhere—Evy, what are you doing!"

But Evolet was gone, back through the cave to where they'd left their mother. He turned the corner suddenly, and came upon the scene, skidding to a halt and shoving one of Lucius's soldiers in the process. He could hear the drone of a helicopter flying low outside, but ignored it, and took in the scene.

Violet was completely surrounded, fighting with the remaining seven of the soldiers, and Lucius. She held them off, smashing dart guns in two and kicking real guns away.

But then, even as Evolet ran to her aid, the inevitable happened. She was hit by a dart—no, two of them.

Evolet saw her waver, saw her fall. His scream was raw.

"*No!*"

A moment later he was among the soldiers. Despite his injured foot, he attacked them ruthlessly, throwing them down and out of his way.

But it couldn't last forever, and suddenly he tripped, slamming down on the rocky cave floor, full onto his face, just when final victory was in sight. And before he could get up, a heavy boot pressed between his shoulders. What with the pain from multiple gunshots at this point, Evolet couldn't move.

He felt the end of a rifle on the back of his head, and froze.

"Stupid," came the Major's voice, laced with contempt. "You asked for this."

"Touch a hair of his head and I will kill you."

Evolet realized with a start that it was his mother's voice, weak but somehow firm.

"Kill me? *You?*"

Lucius started laughing, a horrible, sickening laughter that echoed throughout the cave and in Evolet's tortured mind as well. He kept laughing, louder and louder. And then, suddenly, he stopped.

Evolet held his breath and shut his eyes. He was expecting the Major to either say something more, or to shoot, or both.

He wasn't expecting to suddenly hear two gunshots, almost simultaneous, and then the pressure from the gun and the boot to be suddenly gone. There was a crash as the Major hit the floor, and then a somewhat familiar voice.

"Too late, Major. I should've known."

Incredulous, Evolet lifted his head from the ground and looked towards the doorway, to see Eternyti Schwann standing there, leaning heavily against the wall.

She held a smoking pistol. Blood trickled down from a hole in her torn and dirty scientist's coat.

She looked faintly at Evolet, closed her eyes, and nodded. "Evolet Whyte. I'm sorry."

That was all she said, and all she needed to say. Nodding, Evolet turned— and saw Violet.

She was watching him, too, a peaceful, fond light in her purple eyes. She blinked a couple of times as he dragged himself closer, and then she smiled.

"Evy."

"Mom," he choked out, somehow all the mixed emotions he was feeling coming out with the word.

His eyes filled with tears again. "Mom, you can pull through this."

He felt in vain for his pocket knife, and then realized he was already bleeding in a few places. "I'll give you T4 like Jaz—"

Violet shook her head. "We aren't the same blood type, Evy. It won't work."

He had to wipe his eyes before he could see clearly again, and then it only lasted a moment. He shook his head, and reached out to take his mother's hand, squeezing it tightly. "No, Mom—"

She smiled at him. "You know, Evy, I've always had a price to pay."

"But you're...good now, Mom," Evolet managed to say, his voice cracking. "I didn't trust you. Mom, I'm sorry..."

Shaking her head, Violet half-closed her eyes. "There are better things out there, Evolet," she told him slowly, her voice getting weaker and weaker as she went. "Better than strength, better than power... Worth fighting for, worth dying for. I wish you...happiness and peace. Someday. Take my place... I hope the best for you. Evolet..."

He couldn't stop crying now, especially when her returning squeeze on his hand got weaker and weaker. "Please. Mom. Don't."

It was hard for her to breathe now, and her eyes were almost closed. He doubted she could see him. Evolet gripped her hand until he thought he might break it.

"Little Evolet," Violet whispered, as if in a dream. "Little Trooper. Someday you'll know..."

She was remembering. Her entire life flashed before her eyes—happy child, thoughtless teenager, evil Violet Army leader, reformed young woman... Her marriage to Conner Whyte, motherhood, and the pain she'd felt at leaving her darling eldest behind. The joy she'd had with the youngest three. Watching them grow up... Reunion with Evolet... And now her children were all adults, or young adults.

She had had a mission, and it was done now. All of it was done, she knew. She was finished.

She could go now.

Her eyes opened one last time, and Violet breathed three words before taking a final breath.

"Pray for me."

Evolet stared in speechlessly, and just barely managed to nod. He held his breath as the light died out of his mother's eyes. Watching her chest, Evolet hoped against hope.

Nothing. It was over.

Sitting up, Evolet was convulsed in sobs. No, his mother couldn't be dead. She'd only been with him about six years. He wanted her back. It was too much. And then suddenly, his thoughts stilled. All was quiet.

He opened his eyes, looking directly at his mother's peaceful face. Evolet desperately hoped that she was happy now.

Gently, Evolet reached out and closed her eyes for the last time.

He barely noticed as Jasmine stumbled out of the far cave, took in the scene, and collapsed at Evolet's side, crying harder than he ever had.

"No... Mom... No..."

Evolet let her cry, for what seemed forever. He knew she must be feeling worse than he was. Especially as now the first pangs had gone and been replaced by a dull, constant knot in his chest. His eyes were dry now, and there was a strange feeling of peace.

He could hear the birds chirping outside the cave, and he knew it was over. The fighting, the pain, the heartbreak—it was over. The battle was lost—but no, he realized, the battle was won.

He hugged Jasmine, for what seemed like another forever, and then stood up, took a deep, shuddering breath, and straightened his shoulders. Then he turned towards the cave mouth and began walking. It was a few seconds before his eyes adjusted to the late morning light, and he could see the newcomer; then he stopped.

Evolet didn't know how long the red-haired scientist had been watching them, but she had been. Not Eternyti—Eternyti was on the ground now, her last efforts having proved fatal, it seemed. Scarlet Dawes had finally arrived. She was just standing there, her red and white-streaked hair blowing around her face like Violet's had done not an hour before.

Evolet couldn't say anything, but he didn't need to. Scarlet's face twisted in compassion.

"Evolet Whyte. I'm so sorry."

forty-nine

A week or so later, Evolet was in his and Charles's room at the new house they'd found in Mongolia, sitting on his bed with his eyes closed, holding his face in his hands. He was remembering.

He was dressed all in black. All the Whytes had been, and the Foleys, too. They all missed Violet. Even now, Evolet still felt the horrible, aching loneliness. He was suspicious it would never go away.

But the wound to their family life would heal eventually—at least partly. They would learn to smile again, to laugh, to love. They were safe now, and what with seven hyper-T5 orphans to take care of, life could not be anything but lively. But Evolet knew there would always be that loneliness there, that emptiness. Nothing would ever fill it.

Mom. Why?

Suddenly someone knocked on the door, and Evolet stood up quickly, going over to open it. It was Conner—the wrinkled and gray-haired version of Conner. And he was holding a bundle.

"I think your mother wanted you to have this," he told Evolet simply, his dark, deep blue eyes tired yet hopeful. "You okay, Evy?"

"Yeah. Yeah, I'm okay," Evolet repeated, staring at the small parcel dazedly. "Thanks, Dad." He looked down at his shorter parent, and managed a weak, fake smile.

Conner nodded, and stepped back out into the hallway, leaving without another word. The floorboards creaked as he slowly returned to wherever he'd been, leaving Evolet behind with his bundle.

After a moment or so of hesitation, Evolet elbowed the door, letting it finish closing on its own. Ignoring the fact that it didn't click completely closed, he went back to his bed, and unwrapped the parcel.

It was simply an old, handsewn baby-sized jacket, made of a cool, light purple material with dark blue trimmings. Evolet felt it, moved it around in his hands. On the back of the collar was hand-embroidered the inscription: *Little Trooper.*

Evolet smiled fondly, closing his eyes. He remembered this jacket. If he didn't remember wearing it as a baby, he definitely recalled finding it and wondering about it as a fifteen-year-old. Only five years ago. Now his suspicions were confirmed that it had belonged to him as a baby, and to him only.

Unzipping it carefully, he ran his hands along the inside—and discovered the folded paper inside. Surprised, he drew it out, opening his eyes as a matter of course to read the words on it, in his mother's hand.

Dear Evolet,

I'm writing this to you now, before I leave. I don't have time to write to everyone, so I'll need you to carry on some messages for me. I just hope you see and read this before anything happens and you all leave.

I'm going to destroy Schwann3, and your Aunt Moira is going to give me the coordinates of a safe place she finds, where Arcilla can't hurt us if he ever does find us. Then I'm going to lead Arcilla on a false trail. Whatever you do, don't try to follow me. I told Moira I'm doing this alone, but I don't know if she trusts me. I don't want anyone following me.

I'll probably be back with you all soon, but I just wanted to write this in case I never come back. I love you, Evolet. I know your life has been turned upside down ever since your parents and siblings came back into it. But I want you to know I love you, and I hope someday, somehow, you will find peace and happiness. But remember: life isn't about enjoying happiness now, it's about searching for and earning a better one for later.

Tell your siblings that, and tell them I love them, too. Also, I would have given Conner my last dosage of T4, but I have a crazy feeling I'll need it, so take care of your father, will you? He's a good man, Evolet—better than I ever was. I hope the "cure" won't kill him. But, whatever happens, stay with him, will you? Look after him for me?

Your Aunt is tired, did you know? You need to help and take care of her, too. She's exhausted from dealing with superhumans, and I need you to take on some of that responsibility. You've been doing a good job so far, but you need to do more. Offer to help her. Tell her you'll take the kids out for a day or something, and watch them. Let her rest. She's aged quickly, Evolet...

I have to go now. I have lots more to say but I need to leave before you all wake up. So I'll finish with:

Goodbye, Evolet. God bless and protect you.

I love you—forever.

Violet

Evolet's eyes misted over by the time he finished reading, but he wasn't only sad, he was also aware of a strange feeling of happiness. He knew now. His mother *had* changed since the Purple Blitzkrieg, and she had changed for the good. If only he'd known that sooner! He could've—

He stood up and brushed his sleeve across his eyes.

He'd heard something. No, he'd *sensed* something.

Wheeling around, he discovered it was Michael. The orange-haired superhuman had snuck into the room without a sound and had been watching him. Realizing that the game was up, Michael grinned sheepishly.

"Aunt Moira says it's time for lunch. Will you be coming?" he added anxiously. "You haven't had lunch with us in a long time."

"Four or five days," Evolet corrected, smiling faintly. Carefully he put the jacket and note down on his bed. "Yeah, I'm coming."

"Good," Michael told him, leading the way out of the room.

Halfway down the hallway, he paused, and glanced up at Evolet. "I'm sorry about your mom, by the way. She was a good mom." His blue eyes shone with sincerity.

Evolet nodded slowly.

He looked up and suddenly saw Scarlet standing at the end of the hallway, leaning against the doorway to the dining room. She'd exchanged her scrubs for a plain, ordinary, and simple getup: laced, black knee-high boots, light gray tights, light brown skirt with a darker brown belt, and a light blue blouse with elbow-length sleeves. Her red hair was done up in a bun at the top of her head, the permanently white streak left loose and trimmed as bangs along with a bit of the local red. Her freckled cheeks were slightly pink—she must've just come in from an outside workout.

She grinned at Michael, and then her blue eyes met Evolet's purple ones, and the grin changed slowly to a gentle, sad smile.

"Yeah," Evolet said finally, still looking at Scarlet. He smiled back.

"She was a good mom."

THE END

epilogue

It was a summer day in Mongolia, about two years later. The area was a quiet one: a large, open yard met with trees on all sides, encircling a big brick house with a welcoming aura about it. But in the backyard, it was anything but quiet. Seven children, ranging from the ages of nine to fifteen, were engaged in an intense game of tag, led by a seventeen-year-old boy with longish, curly light blond hair, deep blue eyes, and a narrow, slanted chin. Their laughter rang out to the clear blue skies; the older teenager caught them all, one by one, and then the game began again.

In another part of the yard, two men were engaged in a game of tennis, the younger of the two sometimes turning around to see that the kids were still doing okay—especially if one or two of the younger ones started screaming. He was tall, with curly and thick dark brown hair, and wielded his racquet with an almost careless ease and accuracy. His purple eyes shone in the morning sunlight.

His companion was definitely much older looking; he was a few inches shorter, with wrinkled skin and grayish, whitish hair. Still somehow he fought on gamely, though to move the racquet cost him ten times the energy it did his youthful, energetic opponent. But he kept up both the game and the conversation.

"I wonder what color hair he'll have," the younger man thought aloud. "What do you think?"

"Could be a she, you know, Evolet," Conner Whyte chuckled. "I dunno. Brown does run strong on our side of the family, so maybe brown. Though that's vague."

"It is that," twenty-two-year-old Evolet agreed pensively. He batted the little white tennis ball back across the table. "But red is strong on Scar's side, too."

"I guess so," Conner nodded. "Purple eyes, though, do you think?"

Evolet laughed at the same time as he did. "Yeah, right," he grinned. "*That's* not happening again."

"You never know," Conner told him seriously. "We weren't expecting you to have purple eyes, either."

Evolet smiled. "Well, it's half as likely this time, so…"

He broke off midsentence, drawing breath in sharply as Conner bent nearly double in an effort to get the ball, and didn't stand up immediately. "Dad, are you okay?"

"Y—e—s," Conner returned slowly, still bent. "Yeah, I'm—fine."

Evolet hesitated with his racquet about to drop on the tennis table. "We can finish the game later—"

Suddenly Conner straightened and looked directly at Evolet, shaking his head in disbelief.

"What?" Evolet asked him, worried.

"Evy…"

His deep blue eyes were lit with a strange, new, hopeful light. Slowly Conner's face broke into an incredulous smile.

"Evolet. It's back. It's coming back."

His voice was hushed, but it grew stronger as he gripped the tennis table with superhuman strength. "It's coming back!"

About the Author

Gabrielle Marie Kozak is a 20-year-old author living in the United States. Her debut, the Trooper Series, includes some of her works compiled before graduating high school. A unique writer, Gabrielle successfully writes contemporary fiction, her main theme being that of individual sovereignty refusing to surrender to the restrictive, devastating oppression that surrounds it.

The eldest of nine children, Gabrielle spent almost two years as a religious Sister and now hopes to pursue a Bachelor's Degree in Creative Writing while continuing to captivate readers with her raw, intimate portrayals of the human soul. She lives in Nebraska and loves writing, coffee, and all things Poland.

https://www.gmariaek.com

Also by Gabrielle Marie Kozak

Gabrielle Marie Kozak's works span several different genres, from fantasy legend to psychological thriller! (More coming soon!)

Trooper A1: The Purple Blitzkrieg

Moira Whyte refuses to believe the **bloody evidence** that confirms her brother's death. Instead, she begins to hack into **Encephalon**, the underground network built to **subjugate the entire world.**

She's right. Her brother isn't dead.

He's worse than dead.

Trooper A2: "Little Trooper"

When **Evolet Whyte** first meets his real parents and siblings, they **shatter** his view on life–forever. **His mother has a story.** Does he trust her–or does he believe what **history itself** tells him?

The **truth won't wait** for him to find it in the skyscrapers and the classrooms. It's coming to find him–and it could **destroy** both Evolet and his new-found family.

To survive, Evolet must **discover and awaken** the "Little" Trooper within.